Archer Butler Hulbert

The Future of Road-making in America

Archer Butler Hulbert

The Future of Road-making in America

1st Edition | ISBN: 978-3-75237-943-3

Place of Publication: Frankfurt am Main, Germany

Year of Publication: 2020

Outlook Verlag GmbH, Germany.

Reproduction of the original.

The Future of Road-making in America

BY

ARCHER BUTLER HULBERT

CHAPTER I

THE FUTURE OF ROAD-MAKING IN AMERICA

In introducing the subject of the future of road-making in America, it may first be observed that there is to be a future in road-building on this continent. We have today probably the poorest roads of any civilized nation; although, considering the extent of our roads, which cover perhaps a million and a half miles, we of course have the best roads of any nation of similar age. As we have elsewhere shown, the era of railway building eclipsed the great era of road and canal building in the third and fourth decades of the old century, and it is interesting to note that freight rates on American railways today are cheaper than on any railways in any other country of the world. To move a ton of freight in England one hundred miles today, you pay two dollars and thirty cents; in Germany, two dollars; in France, one dollar and seventy-five cents; in "poor downtrodden" Russia, one dollar and thirty cents. But in America it costs on the average only seventy-two cents. This is good, but it does not by any means answer all the conditions; the average American farm is located today—even with our vast network of railways—at least ten miles from a railroad station. Now railway building has about reached its limit so far as mileage is concerned in this country; in the words of Stuyvesant Fish, president of the Illinois Central Railroad Company, we have "in the United States generally, a sufficiency of railroads." Thus the average farm is left a dozen miles from a railway, and in all probability will be that far away a century from now. And note: seventy-five per cent of the commerce of the world starts for its destination on wagon roads, and we pay annually in the United States six hundred million dollars freightage to get our produce over our highways from the farms to the railways.

Let me restate these important facts: the average American farm is ten miles from a railway; the railways have about reached their limit of growth territorially; and we pay six hundred million dollars every year to get the seventy-five per cent of our raw material and produce from our farms to our railways.

This is the main proposition of the good roads problem, and the reason why the road question is to be one of the great questions of the next half century. The question is, How much can we save of this half a billion dollars, at the least expenditure of money and in the most beneficial way?

In this problem, as in many, the most important phase is the one most difficult to study and most difficult to solve. It is as complex as human life itself. It is the question of good roads as they affect the social and moral life of our rural communities. It is easy to talk of bad roads costing a half billion dollars a year—the answer should be that of Hood's—"O God! that bread should be so dear, and flesh and blood so cheap." You cannot count in terms of the stock exchange the cost to this land of poor roads; for poor roads mean the decay of country living, the abandonment of farms and farm-life, poor schools, poor churches, and homes stricken with a social poverty that drives the young men and girls into the cities. You cannot estimate the cost to this country, in blood, brain, and muscle, of the hideous system of public roads we have possessed in the decade passed. Look at any of our cities to the men who guide the swift rush of commercial, social, and religious affairs and you will find men whose birthplaces are not preparing another such generation of men for the work of the future.

For instance, bad roads and good schools are incompatible. The coming generation of strong men and strong women is crying out now for good roads. "There is a close and permanent relation," said Alabama's superintendent of education, "existing between good public roads and good public schools. There can be no good country schools in the absence of good country roads. Let us be encouraged by this movement looking toward an improvement in road-building and road-working. I see in it a better day for the boys and girls who must look to the country schools for citizenship." "I have been longing for years," said President Jesse of the University of Missouri, "to stump the capital state, if necessary, in favor of the large consolidated schoolhouse rather than the single schoolhouses sitting at the crossroads. But the wagons could not get two hundred yards in most of our counties. Therefore I have had to smother my zeal, hold my tongue, and wait for the consolidated schoolhouse until Missouri wakes to the necessity of good roads. Then not only shall we have consolidated schoolhouses, but also the principal of the school and his wife will live in the school building, or in one close by. The library and reading-room of the school will be the library and reading-room of the neighborhood.... The main assembly room of the consolidated schoolhouse will be an assembly place for public lectures.... I am in favor of free text-books, but I tell you here and now that free text-books are a trifle compared with good roads and the consolidated schoolhouse." It is found that school attendance in states where good roads abound is from twenty-five to fifty per cent greater than in states which have not good roads. How long will it take for the consolidated schoolhouse and increased and regular attendance to be worth half a billion dollars to American men and women of the next generation?

This applies with equal pertinency to what I might call the consolidated church; good roads make it possible for a larger proportion of country residents to enjoy the superior advantages of the splendid city churches; in fact good roads have in certain instances been held guilty of destroying the little country church. This could be true within only a small radius of the cities, and the advantages to be gained outweigh, I am sure, the loss occasioned by the closing of small churches within a dozen miles of our large towns and cities—churches which, in many cases, have only occasional services and are a constant financial drain on the city churches. Farther out in the country, good roads will make possible one strong, healthy church where perhaps half a dozen weak organizations are made to lead a precarious existence because bad roads make large congregations impossible throughout the larger part of the year. This also applies to city schools, libraries, hospitals, museums, and lyceums. Good roads will place these advantages within reach of millions of country people who now know little or nothing of them. Once beyond driving distance of the cities, good roads will make it possible for thousands to reach the suburban railways and trolley lines. Who can estimate in mere dollars these advantages to the quality of American citizenship a century hence? American farms are taxed by the government and pay one-half of the seven hundred million dollars it takes yearly to operate this government. After receiving one-half, what per cent does the government return to them? Only ten per cent. Ninety per cent goes to the direct or indirect benefit of those living in our cities. Where does the government build its fine buildings, where does it spend its millions on rivers and harbors? How much does it expend to ease this burden of six hundred millions which lies so largely on the farmers of America? A few years ago a law was passed granting $50,000 to investigate a plan to deliver mail on rural delivery routes to our farmers and country residents. The law was treated about as respectfully as the long-headed Jesse Hawley who wrote a series of articles advocating the building of the Erie Canal; a certain paper printed a few of them, but the editor sent the remainder back saying he could not use them— they were making his sheet an object of ridicule. Eighteen years later the canal was built and in the first year brought in a revenue of $492,664. So with the first Rural Free Delivery appropriation—the postmaster general to whose hands that first $50,000 was entrusted for experimental purposes, refused to try it and sent the money back to the treasury. Today the Rural Free Delivery is an established fact, of immeasurable benefit; and if any of the appropriations for it are not expended it is not because they are being sent back to the treasury by scrupulous officials. Rural delivery routes diverge from our towns and cities and give the country people the advantages of a splendid post office system. Good roads to these cities would give them a score of advantages where now they have but this one. Like rural delivery it may seem impracticable, but in a short space of time America will leap forward in the front rank of the nations in point of good highways.

An execrable road system, besides bringing poor schools and poor churches, has rendered impossible any genuine community of social interests among country people. At the very season when the farm work is light and social intercourse feasible, at that season the highways have been impassable. To this and the poor schools and churches may be attributed the saddest and really most costly social revolution in America in the past quarter of a century. The decline of country living must in the nature of things prove disastrously costly to any nation. "The roar of the cannon and the gleam of swords," wrote that brilliant apostle of outdoor life, Dr. W. H. H. Murray, "is less significant than the destruction of New England homesteads, the bricking up of New England fireplaces and the doing away with the New England well-sweep; for these show a change in the nature of the circulation itself, and prove that the action of the popular heart has been interrupted, modified and become altogether different from what it was." In the popular mind the benefits of country living are common only as a fad; the boy who goes to college and returns to the farm again is one of a thousand. Who wants to be landlocked five months of the year, without social advantages? Good roads, in one generation, would accomplish a social revolution throughout the United States that would greatly tend to better our condition and brighten the prospect of future strength. President Winston of the North Carolina State College of Agriculture said: "It might be demonstrated beyond a reasonable doubt that bad roads are unfavorable to matrimony and increase of population." Seven of the most stalwart lads and beautiful lasses of Greece were sent each year to Crete to be sacrificed to the Minotaur; bad roads in America send thousands of boys and girls into our cities to the Minotaurs of evil because conditions in the country do not make for the social happiness for which they naturally yearn.

Thus we may hint at the greater, more serious, phase of the road problem. Beside it, the financial feature of the problem can have no place; the farm has been too much to the American nation, its product of boys and girls has been too eternally precious to the cause of liberty for which our nation stands, to permit a system of highways on this continent which will make it a place where now in the twentieth century foreigners, only, can be happy. The sociological side of the road question is of more moment today in this country, so far as the health of our body politic in the future is concerned, than nine-tenths of the questions most prominent in the two political platforms that come annually before the people.

William Jennings Bryan, when addressing the Good Roads Convention at St. Louis in 1903, said:

"It is a well-known fact, or a fact easily ascertained, that the people in the country, while paying their full share of county, state, and federal taxes, receive as a rule only the general benefits of government, while the people in the cities have, in addition to the protection afforded by the Government, the advantage arising from the expenditure of public moneys in their midst. The county seat of a county, as a rule, enjoys the refreshing influence of an expenditure of county money out of proportion to its population. The capital of a state and the city where the state institutions are located, likewise receive the benefit of an expenditure of public money out of proportion to their population. When we come to consider the distribution of the moneys collected by the Federal Government, we find that the cities, even in a larger measure, monopolize the incidental benefits that arise from the expenditure of public moneys.

"The appropriations of the last session of Congress amounted to $753,484,018, divided as follows:

Agriculture	$ 5,978,160
Army	78,138,752
Diplomatic and consular service	1,968,250
District of Columbia	8,647,497
Fortifications	7,188,416
Indians	8,512,950
Legislative, executive, and judicial departments	27,595,958
Military Academy	563,248
Navy	81,877,291
Pensions	139,847,600
Post Office Department	153,401,409
Sundry Civil	82,722,955
Deficiencies	21,561,572
Permanent annual	132,589,820
Miscellaneous	3,250,000

"It will be seen that the appropriation for the Department of Agriculture was insignificant when compared with the total appropriations—less than one per cent. The appropriations for the Army and Navy alone amounted to twenty-five times the sum appropriated for the Department of Agriculture. An analysis of the expenditures of the Federal Government will show that an exceedingly small proportion of the money raised from all the people gets back to the farmers directly; how much returns indirectly it is impossible to say, but certain it is that the people who live in the cities receive by far the major part of the special benefits that come from the showering of public money upon the community. The advantage obtained locally from government expenditures is so great that the contests for county seats and state capitals usually exceed in interest, if not in bitterness, the contests over political principles and policies. So great is the desire to secure an appropriation of money for local purposes that many will excuse a Congressman's vote on either side of any question if he can but secure the expenditure of a large amount of public money in his district.

"I emphasize this because it is a fact to which no reference has been made. The point is that the farmer not only pays his share of the taxes, but more than his share, yet very little of what he pays gets back to him.

"People in the city pay not only less than their share, as a rule, but get back practically all of the benefits that come from the expenditure of the people's money. Let me show you what I mean when I say that the farmer pays more than his share. The farmer has visible property, and under any form of direct taxation visible property pays more than its share. Why? Because the man with visible property always pays. If he has an acre of land the assessor can find it. He can count the horses and cattle.... The farmer has nothing that escapes taxation; and, in all direct taxation, he not only pays on all he has, but the farmer who has visible property has to pay a large part of the taxes that ought to be paid by the owners of invisible property, who escape taxation. I repeat, therefore, that the farmer not only pays more than his share of all direct taxation, but that when you come to expend public moneys you do not spend them on the farms, as a rule. You spend them in the cities, and give the incidental benefits to the people who live in the cities.

"When indirect taxation is considered, the farmer's share is even more, because when you come to collect taxes through indirection and on consumption, you make people pay not in proportion to what they have but in proportion to what they need, and God has so made us that the farmer needs as much as anybody else, even though he may not have as much with which to supply his needs as other people. In our indirect taxation, therefore, for the support of the Federal Government, the farmers pay even more out of proportion to their wealth and numbers. We should remember also that when we collect taxes through consumption we make the farmer pay not only on that which is imported, but upon much of that which is produced at home. Thus the farmer's burden is not measured by what the treasury receives, but is frequently many times what the treasury receives. Thus under indirect taxation the burden upon the farmer is greater than it ought to be; yet when you trace the expenditure of public moneys distributed by the Federal Government you find that even in a larger measure special benefits go to the great cities and not to the rural communities.

"The improvement of the country roads can be justified also on the ground that the farmer, the first and most important of the producers of wealth, ought to be in position to hold his crop and market it at the most favorable opportunity, whereas at present he is virtually under compulsion to sell it as soon as it is matured, because the roads may become impassable at any time during the fall, winter, or spring. Instead of being his own warehouseman, the farmer is compelled to employ middlemen, and share with them the profits upon his labor. I believe, as a matter of justice to the farmer, he ought to have roads that will enable him to keep his crop and take it to the market at the best time, and not place him in a position where they can run down the price of what he has to sell during the months he must sell, and then, when he has disposed of it, run the price up and give the speculator what the farmer ought to have. The farmer has a right to insist upon roads that will enable him to go to town, to church, to the schoolhouse, and to the homes of his neighbors, as occasion may require; and, with the extension of rural mail delivery, he has additional need for good roads in order that he may be kept in communication with the outside world, for the mail routes follow the good roads.

"A great deal has been said, and properly so, in regard to the influence of good roads upon education. In the convention held at Raleigh, North Carolina, the account of which I had the pleasure of reading, great emphasis was placed upon the fact that you can not have a school system such as you ought to have unless the roads are in condition for the children to go to school. While we are building great libraries in the great cities we do not have libraries in the country; and there ought to be a library in every community. Instead of laying upon the farmer the burden of buying his own books, we ought to make it possible for the farmers to have the same opportunity as the people in the city to use books in common, and thus economize on the expense of a library. I agree with Professor Jesse in regard to the consolidation of schoolhouses in such a way as to give the child in the country the same advantages which the child in the city has. We have our country schools, but it is impossible in any community to have a well-graded school with only a few pupils, unless you go to great expense. In cities, when a child gets through the graded school he can remain at home, and, without expense to himself or his parents, go on through the high school. But if the country boy or girl desires to go from the graded school to the high school, as a rule it is necessary to go to the county seat and there board with some one; so the expense to the country child is much greater than to the child in the city. I was glad, therefore, to hear Professor Jesse speak of such a consolidation of schools as will give to the children in the country advantages equal to those enjoyed by the children of the city.

"And as you study this subject, you find it reaches out in every direction; it touches us at every vital point. What can be of more interest to us than the schooling of our children? What can be of more interest to every parent than bringing the opportunity of educational instruction within the reach of every child? It does not matter whether a man has children himself or not.... Every citizen of a community is interested in the intellectual life of that community. Sometimes I have heard people complain that they were overburdened with taxes for the education of other people's children. My friends, the man who has no children can not afford to live in a community where there are children growing up in ignorance; the man with none has the same duty as the man with many, barring the personal pride of the parent. I say, therefore, that anything that contributes to the general diffusion of knowledge, anything that makes more educated boys and girls throughout our country, is a matter of intense interest to every citizen, whether he be the father of a family or not; whether he lives in the country or in the town.

"And ought not the people have the opportunity to attend church? I am coming to believe that what we need in this country, even more than education of the intellect, is the education of the moral side of our nature. I believe, with Jefferson, that the church and the state should be separate. I believe in religious freedom, and I would not have any man's conscience fettered by act of law; but I do believe that the welfare of this nation demands that man's moral nature shall be educated in keeping with his brain and with his body. In fact, I have come to define civilization as the harmonious development of the body, the mind, and the heart. We make a mistake if we believe that this nation can fulfil its high destiny and mission either with mere athletes or mere scholars. We need the education of the moral sense; and if these good roads will enable men, women, and children to go more frequently to church, and there hear expounded the gospel and receive inspiration therefrom, that alone is reason enough for good roads.

"There is a broader view of this question, however, that deserves consideration. The farm is, and always has been, conspicuous because of the physical development it produces, the intellectual strength it furnishes, and the morality it encourages. The young people in the country find health and vigor in the open air and in the exercise which farm life gives; they acquire habits of industry and economy; their work gives them opportunity for thought and reflection; their contact with nature teaches them reverence, and their environment promotes good habits. The farms supply our colleges with their best students and they also supply our cities with leaders in business and professional life. In the country there is neither great wealth nor great poverty —'the rich and the poor meet together' and recognize that 'the Lord is the father of them all.' There is a fellowship, and, to use the word in its broadest sense, a democracy in the country that is much needed today to temper public opinion and protect the foundations of free government. A larger percentage of the people in the country than in the city study public questions, and a smaller percentage are either corrupt or are corrupted. It is important, therefore, for the welfare of our government and for the advancement of our civilization that we make life upon the farm as attractive as possible. Statistics have shown the constant increase in the urban population and the constant decrease in the rural population from decade to decade. Without treading upon controversial ground or considering whether this trend has been increased by legislation hostile to the farm, it will be admitted that the government is in duty bound to guard jealously the interests of the rural population, and, as far as it can, make farm life inviting. In the employment of modern conveniences the city has considerably outstripped the country, and naturally so, for in a densely populated community the people can by coöperation supply themselves with water, light, and rapid transit at much smaller cost than they can in a sparsely settled country. But it is evident that during the last few years much has been done to increase the comforts of the farm. In the first place, the rural mail delivery has placed millions of farmers in daily communication with the world. It has brought not only the letter but the newspaper to the door. Its promised enlargement and extension will make it possible for the wife to order from the village store and have her purchases delivered by the mail-carrier. The telephone has also been a great boon to the farmer. It lessens by one-half the time required to secure a physician in case of accident or illness—an invention which every mother can appreciate. The extension of the electric-car line also deserves notice. It is destined to extend the borders of the city and to increase the number of small farms at the expense of flats and tenement houses. The suburban home will bring light and hope to millions of children.

"But after all this, there still remains a pressing need for better country roads. As long as mud placed an embargo upon city traffic, the farmer could bear his mud-made isolation with less complaint, but with the improvement of city streets and with the establishment of parks and boulevards, the farmer's just demands for better roads find increasing expression."

The late brilliant congressman, Hon. Thomas H. Tongue of Oregon, left on record a few paragraphs on the sociological effect of good roads that ought to be preserved:

"Good roads do not concern our pockets only. They may become the instrumentalities for improved health, increased happiness and pleasure, for refining tastes, strengthening, broadening, and elevating the character. The toiler in the great city must have rest and recreation. Old and young, and especially the young, with character unformed, must and will sweeten the daily labor with some pleasure. It is not the hours of industry, but the hours devoted to pleasure, that furnish the devil his opportunity. It is not while we are at work but while we are at play that temptations steal over the senses, put conscience to sleep, despoil manhood, and destroy character. Healthful and innocent recreations and pleasure are national needs and national blessings. They are among the most important instrumentalities of moral reform. They are as essential to purity of mind and soul as to healthfulness of body. Out beyond the confines of the city, with its dust and dirt and filth, morally and physically, these are to be found, and good roads help to find them. What peace and inspiration may come from flowers and music, brooks and waterfalls! How the mountains pointing heavenward, yesterday battling with storms, today bathed with sunshine, bid you stand firm, walk erect, look upward, cherish hope, and for light and guidance to call upon the Creator of all light and of all wisdom! How such scenes as these kindle the imagination of the poet, quicken and enlarge the conception of the artist, fire the soul of the orator, purify and elevate us all! But if love of action rather than contemplation and reflection tempts you, how the blood thrills and the spirits rise as one springs lightly into the saddle, caresses the slender neck of an equine beauty, grasps firmly the reins, bids farewell to the impurities of the city, and dashes into the hills and the valleys and the mountains to commune with nature and nature's God. Or what joy more exquisite than with pleasant companionship to dash along the smooth highway, drawn by a noble American trotter? What poor city scenes can so inspire poetic feeling, can so increase the love of the beautiful, can so elevate and broaden and strengthen the character, and so inspire us with reverence for the great Father of us all? But for the full enjoyment of such pleasures good roads are indispensable.

"Another blessing to come with good roads will be the stimulus and encouragements to rural life, farm life. The present tendency of population to rush into the great cities makes neither for the health nor the character, the intelligence nor the morals of the nation. It has been said that no living man can trace his ancestry on both sides to four generations of city residents. The brain and the brawn and the morals of the city are constantly replenished from the country. The best home life is upon the farm, and the most sacred thing in America is the American home. It lies at the foundation of our institutions, of our health, of our character, our prosperity, our happiness, here and hereafter. The snares and pitfalls set for our feet are not near the home. The pathways upon which stones are hardest and thorns sharpest are not those that lead to the sacred spot hallowed by a father's love and a mother's prayers. The bravest and best of men, the purest and holiest women, are those who best love, cherish, and protect the home. God guard well the American home, and this done, come all the powers of darkness and they shall not prevail against us. Fatherhood and motherhood are nowhere more sacred, more holy, or better beloved than upon the farm. The ties of brotherhood and sisterhood are nowhere more sweet or tender. The fair flower of patriotism there reaches its greatest perfection. Every battlefield that marks the world's progress, the victory of liberty over tyranny or right over wrong, has been deluged with the blood of farmers. He evades neither the taxgatherer nor the recruiting officer. He shirks the performance of no public duty. In the hour of its greatest needs our country never called for help upon its stalwart yeomen when the cry was unheeded. The sons and daughters of American farmers are filling the seminaries and colleges and universities of the land. From the American farm home have gone in the past, as they are going now, leaders in literature, the arts and sciences, presidents of great universities, the heads of great industrial enterprises, governors of states, and members of Congress. They have filled the benches of the supreme court, the chairs of the cabinet, and the greatest executive office in the civilized world. Our greatest jurist, our greatest soldier, our greatest orators, Webster and Clay, our three greatest presidents, Washington, Lincoln, and McKinley, were the product of rural homes. The great presidents which Virginia has given to the nation, whose monuments are all around us, whose remains rest in your midst, whose fame is immortal, drew life and inspiration from rural homes. The typical American today is the American farmer. The city life, with its bustle and stir, its hurry and rush, its feverish anxiety for wealth, position, and rank in society, its fretting over ceremonies and precedents, is breaking down the health and intellect and the morals of its inhabitants. These must be replenished from the rural home. Whatever shall tend to create a love for country life, to decrease the rush for the city, instil a desire to dwell in the society of nature, will make for the health, the happiness, the refinement, the moral and intellectual improvement of the people. Nothing will contribute more to this than the improvement of our common roads, to facilitate the means of communication between one section of the country and the other, and between all and the city."

Turning now from the high plane of the social and moral effect of good roads, let us look at the financial side of the question.

Good roads pay well. In urging good roads in Virginia, an official of the Southern Railway said that if good roads improved the value of lands only one dollar per acre, the gain to the state by the improvement of all the roads would be twenty-five million dollars. Yet this is an inconceivably low estimate; lands upon improved roads advance in value from four to twenty dollars per acre. Virginia could therefore expect a benefit from improved highways of at least one hundred million dollars—more than enough to improve her roads many times over. Indeed this matter of the increase in value of land occasioned by good roads can hardly be overestimated. Near all of our large towns and cities the land will advance until it is worth per foot what it was formerly worth per acre. Take Mecklenburg County, North Carolina. Beginning in 1880 to macadamize three or four miles of road a year with an annual fund of $10,000, the county now has over a hundred miles of splendid roads; the county seat has increased in population from 5,000 to 30,000. "I know of a thirty-acre farm," said President Barringer of the University of Virginia, a native of that county, "that cost ten dollars an acre, and forty-six dollars an acre has been refused for it, and yet not a dollar has been put on it, not even to fertilize it. Some of the farms five and six miles from town have quadruled in value." In Alabama the same thing has been found true. "The result of building these roads," said Mayor Drennen of Birmingham, "is that the property adjoining them has more than doubled in value." That wise financier, D. F. Francis, President of the Louisiana Purchase Exposition, when suggesting that Missouri would do well to bond herself for one hundred million to build good roads, said: "The average increase in the value of the lands in Missouri would be at least five dollars per acre." Taking President Francis at his word, the difference between the value of Missouri before and after the era of good roads would buy up the four hundred and eighty-four state banks in Missouri eleven times over. What President Francis estimates Missouri would be worth with good roads over and above what her farms are now worth would buy all the goods that the city of St. Louis produces in a year. In other words, the estimated gain to Missouri would be more than two hundred and twenty million dollars.

Passing the increased value of lands, look at the equally vital question of increased values of crops. Take first the crops that would be raised on lands not cultivated today but which would be cultivated in a day of good roads. Look at Virginia, where only one-third of the land is being cultivated; the value of crops which it is certain would ultimately be raised on land that is now unproductive would amount to at least sixty million dollars. The general passenger agent of the Oregon Railway and Navigation Company said recently that his lines were crying out for wheat to ship to China; "we have about reached the limit of our facilities; twelve or fifteen miles is the only distance farmers can afford to haul their wheat to us. Make it possible for them to haul it double that distance and you will double the business of our railway." And the business of local nature done by a railroad is a good criterion of the prosperity of the country in which it operates.

Crops now raised on lands within reach of railways would of course be enhanced in value by good roads; more loads could be taken at less cost;

weather interferences would not enter into the question. But of more moment perhaps than anything else, a vast amount of land thus placed within quick reach of our towns and cities would be given over to gardening for city markets, a line of agriculture immensely profitable, as city people well know. "The citizens of Birmingham," said the mayor of that city, "enjoy the benefits of fresh products raised on the farms along these [improved] roads. The dairymen, the truck farmers, and others … are put in touch with our markets daily, thereby receiving the benefits of any advance in farm products."

Poor roads are like the interest on a debt, and they are working against one all the time. It is noticeable that when good roads are built, farmers, who are always conservative, adjust themselves more readily to conditions. They are in touch with the world and they feel more keenly its pulse, much to their advantage. Too many farmers, damned by bad roads, are guilty of the faults of which Birmingham's mayor accused Alabama planters: "The farmers in this section," he said, "are selling cotton today for less than seven cents per pound, while they could have sold Irish potatoes within the past few months at two dollars per bushel." Farmers over the entire country are held to be slow in taking advantage of their whole opportunities; bad roads take the life out of them and out of their horses; they think somewhat as they ride—desperately slow; and they will not think faster until they ride faster. It is said that a man riding on a heavy southern road saw a hat in the mud; stopping to pick it up he was surprised to find a head of hair beneath it: then a voice came out of the ground: "Hold on, boss, don't take my hat; I've got a powerful fine mule down here somewhere if I can ever get him out." You can write and speak to farmers until doomsday about taking quick advantage of the exigencies of the markets that are dependent on them, but if they have to hunt for their horses in a hog-wallow road all your talk will be in vain.

When we seriously face the question of how a fine system of highways is to be built in this country, it is found to be a complex problem. For about ten years now it has been seriously debated, and these years have seen a large advance; until now the problem has become almost national.

One great fundamental idea has been proposed and is now generally accepted by all who have paid the matter any attention, and that is that those who live along our present roads cannot be expected to bear the entire cost of building good roads. This may be said to be settled and need no debate. Practically all men are agreed that the rural population should not bear the entire expense of an improvement of which they, however, are to be the chief beneficiaries; the state itself, in all its parts, benefits from the improved conditions which follow improved roads, and should bear a portion of the expense. Do not think that city people escape the tax of bad roads. In St.

Louis four hundred thousand people consume five hundred tons of produce every day. The cost of hauling this produce over bad roads averages twenty-five cents per mile and over good roads about ten cents per mile, making a difference of fifteen cents per mile per ton. For five hundred tons, hauled from farms averaging ten miles distance, this would be seven hundred and fifty dollars per day, or a quarter of a million dollars a year—enough to build fifty miles of macadamized road a year. The farmers shift as much as they can of their heavy tax on the city people—the consumer pays the freight. Everybody is concerned in the "mud-tax" of bad roads.

And so what is known as the "state aid" plan has become popular. By this plan the state pays a fixed part of the cost of building roads out of the general fund raised by taxation of all the people and all the property in the state. Under these circumstances corporations, railroads, and the various representatives of the concentrated wealth of the cities all contribute to this fund. The funds are expended in rural districts and are supplemented by money raised by local taxation.

The state of New York, which has a good system, pays one-half of the good roads fund; each county pays thirty-five per cent, and the township fifteen per cent. Pennsylvania has appropriated at one time six and a half millions as a good roads fund. The new Ohio law apportions the cost of new roads as follows: The state pays twenty-five per cent, the townships twenty-five per cent, and the county fifty per cent. Of the twenty-five per cent paid by the townships fifteen per cent is to be paid by owners of abutting property and ten per cent by the township as a whole. In New Jersey, which has a model system of road-building and many model roads, the state pays a third, the county a third, and the property owners a third.

A more recent theory in American road-building which has been advanced is a plan of national aid.[1] This is no new thing in America, though it has been many years since the government has paid attention to roadways. In the early days the wisest of our statesmen advocated large plans of internal improvement; one great national road, as we have seen, was built by the War Department from the Potomac almost to the Mississippi, through Wheeling, Columbus, Indianapolis and Vandalia, at a cost of over six million dollars. And this famous national road was built, in part, upon an earlier pathway, cut through Ohio by Ebenezer Zane in 1796, also at the order of Congress, and for which he received grants of land which formed the nucleus of the three thriving Ohio cities, Zanesville, Lancaster, and Chillicothe. The constitutionality of road-building by the government was questioned by some, but that clause granting it the right to establish post-offices and post roads "must, in every view, be a harmless power," said James Madison, "and may perhaps, by judicious management, become productive of great public conveniency. Nothing which tends to facilitate the intercourse between the states can be deemed unworthy of the public care."[2] But the government was interested not only in building roads but in many other phases of public improvement; it took stock in the Chesapeake and Ohio Canal; Congress voted $30,000 to survey the Chesapeake and Ohio Canal route, and the work was done by government engineers. When railways superseded highways, the government was almost persuaded to complete the old National Road with rails and ties instead of broken stone. When the Erie Canal was proposed, a vast scheme of government aid was favored by leading statesmen;[3] the government has greatly assisted the western railways by gigantic grants of land worth one hundred and thirty-eight million dollars. The vast funds of private capital that have been seeking investment in this country, at first in turnpike, plank, and macadamized roads, then in canals, and later in railways, has rendered government aid comparatively unnecessary. In the last few years the only work of internal improvement aided by the government is the improvement of the rivers and harbors, which for 1904 takes over fifty millions of revenue a year. The sum of $130,565,485 has been well spent on river and harbor improvement in the past seven years. Not only are the great rivers, such as the Ohio and Mississippi, improved, but lesser streams. A short time ago I made a journey of one hundred miles down the Elk River in West Virginia in a boat eleven inches deep and twelve feet long; a channel all the way down had been made about two feet wide by picking out the stones; the United States did this at an expense of fifteen hundred dollars. The groceries and dry goods for thousands were poled up that river in dug-outs through that two-foot channel. I doubt if a two-wheel vehicle could traverse the road which runs throughout that valley, but I know a four-wheel vehicle could not.

The advocates of national aid urge the right to establish post roads; "I had an ancestor in the United States Senate," said ex-Senator Butler of South Carolina, "who refused to vote a dollar for the improvement of Charleston Harbor; but almost the first act of my official life was to get an appropriation of two hundred and fifty thousand for that purpose. There is as ample constitutional warrant for the improvement of public roads out of the United States Treasury—as large as there is for the improvement of rivers and harbors, or for the support of the agricultural colleges."

"But few judicial opinions have been rendered on this subject. In the case of Dickey against the Turnpike Company, the Kentucky court of appeals decided that the power given to Congress by the constitution to establish post roads enabled them to make, repair, keep open, and improve post roads when they shall deem the exercise of the power expedient. But in the exercise of the right of eminent domain on this subject the United States has no right to adopt and use roads, bridges, or ferries constructed and owned by states, corporations, and individuals without their consent or without making to the parties concerned just compensation. If the United States elects to use such accommodations, it stands upon the same footing and is subject to the same tolls and regulations as a private individual. It has been asserted that Jefferson was opposed to the appropriation of money for internal improvements, but, in 1808, in writing to Mr. Lieper, he said, 'Give us peace until our revenues are liberated from debt, ... and then during peace we may chequer our whole country with canals, roads, etc.' Writing to J. W. Eppes in 1813 he says, 'The fondest wish of my heart ever was that the surplus portion of these taxes destined for the payment of the Revolutionary debt should, when that object is accomplished, be continued by annual or biennial reënactments and applied in times of peace to the improvement of our country by canals, roads, and useful institutions.' Congress has always claimed the power to lay out, construct, and improve post roads with the assent of the states through which they pass; also, to open, construct, and improve military roads on like terms; and the right to cut canals through the several states with their consent for the purpose of promoting and securing internal commerce and for the safe and economical transportation of military stores in times of war. The president has sometimes objected to the exercise of this constitutional right, but Congress has never denied it. Cooley, the highest authority on constitutional law, says:

"'Every road within a State, including railroads, canals, turnpikes, and navigable streams, existing or created within a State, becomes a post-road, whenever by law or by the action of the Post-Office Department provision is made for the transportation of the mail upon or over it. Many statesmen and jurists have contended that the power comprehends the laying out and construction of any roads which Congress may deem proper and needful for the conveyance of the mails, and keeping them repaired for the purpose.'"[4]

It has been many years since the United States government was interested considerably in mail routes on the roadways of this country; in the past half century the government has spent but one hundred thousand dollars for the improvement of mail roads. The new era of rural delivery brings a return, in one sense, of the old stagecoach days. A thousand country roads are now used daily by government mail-carriers, but the government demands that the roads used be kept in good condition by the local authorities. Thus the situation is reversed; instead of holding it to be the duty of the government to deliver mail in rural districts, Congress holds that the debt is on the other side and that, in return for the boon of rural delivery, the rural population must make good roads. Madison well saw that government improvement of roads as mail routes would be of great general benefit; for in *The Federalist* he adds that the power "may perhaps by judicious management become productive of great public conveniency."

A GOOD-ROADS TRAIN

[*The Southern Roadway's good-roads train, October 29, 1901, consisting of two coaches for officials and road experts and ten cars of road machinery; for itinerary through Virginia, North Carolina. Tennessee, Alabama, and Georgia*]

One great work the government has done and is doing. It has founded an Office of Public Road Inquiries (described elsewhere) at Washington, and under the efficient management of Hon. Martin Dodge and Maurice O. Eldridge a great work of education has been carried on—samples of good roads have been built, good road trains have been sent out by the Southern Railway and the Illinois Central into the South, a laboratory has been established at Washington, under the efficient charge of Professor L. W. Page, for the testing of materials free of charge, and a great deal of road information has been published and sent out.

The Brownlow Bill, introduced into Congress at the last session, is the latest plan of national aid, and is thus described by Hon. Martin Dodge of the Office of Public Road Inquiries:

"The bill provides for an appropriation of twenty million dollars. This is to be used only in connection and coöperation with the various states or civil subdivisions of states that may make application to the General Government for the purpose of securing its aid to build certain roads. The application must be made for a specific road to be built, and the state or county making the application must be ready to pay half of the cost, according to the plans and specifications made by the General Government. In no case can any state or any number of counties within the state receive any greater proportion of the twenty million dollars than the population of the state bears to the population of the United States.

"In other words, all of the plans must originate in the community. The bill does not provide that the United States shall go forward and say a road shall be built here or a road shall be built there. The United States shall hold itself in readiness, when requested to do so, to coöperate with those who have selected a road they desire to build, provided they are ready and willing to pay one-half the cost. Then, if the road is a suitable one and is approved by the government authorities, they go forward and build that road, each contributing one-half of the expense. In order to prevent the state losing jurisdiction of the road, it is provided that it may go forward and build the road if it will accept the government engineer's estimate. For instance, if a state or county asks for ten miles of road, the estimated cost of which is thirty thousand dollars, and the state or county officials say they are willing to undertake the work for thirty thousand dollars, the government authorizes them to go ahead and build that road according to specifications, and when it is finished the government will pay the fifteen thousand dollars. If the state or county does not wish to take the contract, the General Government will advertise and give it to the lowest bidder, and will pay its contributory share and the other party will pay its contributory share.

"It is no part of the essential principle involved in this national aid plan that the exact proportion should be fifty per cent on each side. Any other figure can be adopted. Some think ten per cent is sufficient; some think thirty-three and one-third is the proper percentage; others think twenty-five per cent only should be paid by the government, twenty-five per cent by the state, twenty-five per cent by the county, and twenty-five per cent by the township. The one idea that seems to be generally accepted is that the government should do something."

Thus the interest in the great question is beginning to forge to the front; through the Office of Public Road Inquiries a great deal of information is being circulated touching all phases of the question. There is a fine spirit of independence displayed by the leaders of the movement; no one plan is over-urged; the situation is such that the final concerted popular action will come from the real governing power—the people. When they demand that the United States shall not have the poorest rural roads of any civilized and some uncivilized nations, we as a nation will hasten into the fore front and finally lead the world in this vital department of civic life, as we are leading it in so many other departments today.

SAMPLE STEEL TRACK FOR COMMON ROADS

[On the driver's right is seated Hon. Martin Dodge, since 1898 Director of the Office of Public Road Inquiries]

FOOTNOTES:

[1] See *post*, pp. 68-80.

[2] *The Federalist*, p. 198.

[3] *Historic Highways of America*, vol. xiv, p. 57.

[4] Thomas M. Cooley, *Constitutional Law* (Boston, 1891), pp. 85-86.

CHAPTER II

GOVERNMENT COÖPERATION IN OBJECT-LESSON ROAD WORK[5]

In a government having a composite nature like that of the United States it is not always easy to determine just what share the General Government, the state government, and the local government should respectively take in carrying out highway work, though it is generally admitted that there should be coöperation among them all.

In the early history of the Republic the National Government itself laid out and partially completed a great national system of highways connecting the East with the West, and the capital of the nation with its then most distant possessions. Fourteen million dollars in all was appropriated by acts of Congress to be devoted to this purpose, an amount almost equal to that paid for the Louisiana Purchase. In other words, it cost the government substantially as much to make that territory accessible as to purchase it; and what is true of that territory in its larger sense is also true in a small way of nearly every tract of land that is opened up and used for the purposes of civilization; that is to say, it will cost as much to build up, improve, and maintain the roads of any given section of the country as the land in its primitive condition is worth; and the same rule will apply in most cases after the land value has advanced considerably beyond that of its primitive condition. It is a general rule that the suitable improvement of a highway within reasonable limitations will double the value of the land adjacent to it. Seven million dollars, half of the total sum appropriated by acts of Congress for the national road system, was devoted to building the Cumberland Road from Cumberland, Maryland, to St. Louis, Missouri, the most central point in the great Louisiana Purchase, and seven hundred miles west of Cumberland. The total cost of this great road was wholly paid out of the United States Treasury, and though never fully completed on the western end, it is the longest straight road ever built by any government. It passes through the capitals of Ohio, Indiana, and Illinois, and the cost per mile was, approximately, ten thousand dollars. It furnishes the only important instance the country has ever had of the General Government providing a highway at its own expense. The plan, however, was never carried to completion, and since its abandonment two generations ago, the people of the different states have provided their own highways. For the most part they have delegated their powers either to individuals, companies, or corporations to build toll roads, or to the minor political subdivisions and municipalities to build free roads.

With the passing of the toll-road system, the withdrawal of the General Government from the field of actual road construction, and the various state governments doing little or nothing, the only remaining active agent occupying the entire great field is the local government in each community; and while these various local governments have done and are still doing the best they can under the circumstances, there is great need that their efforts should be supplemented, their revenues enlarged, and their skill in the art of road construction increased.

The skill of the local supervisor was sufficient in primitive times, so long as his principal duties consisted in clearing the way of trees, logs, stumps, and other obstructions, and shaping the earth of which the roadbed was composed into a little better form than nature had left it; and the resources at his command were sufficient so long as he was authorized to call on every able-bodied male citizen between twenty-one and forty-five years of age to do ten days' labor annually on the road, especially when the only labor expected was that of dealing with the material found on the spot. But with the changed conditions brought about by the more advanced state of civilization, after the rights of way have been cleared of their obstructions and the earth roads graded into the form of turnpikes, it became necessary to harden their surfaces with material which often must be brought from distant places. In order to accomplish this, expert skill is required in the selection of materials, money instead of labor is required to pay for the cost of transportation, and machinery must be substituted for the hand processes and primitive methods heretofore employed in order to crush the rock and distribute it in the most economical manner on the roadbed. Skill and machinery are also required to roll and consolidate the material so as to form a smooth, hard surface and a homogeneous mass impervious to water.

The local road officer now not only finds himself deficient in skill and the proper kind of resources, but he discovers in many cases that the number of persons subject to his call for road work has greatly diminished. The great cities of the North have absorbed half of the population in all the states north of the Ohio and east of the Mississippi, and those living in these great cities are not subject to the former duties of working the roads, nor do they pay any compensation in money in lieu thereof. So the statute labor has not only become unsuitable for the service to be performed, but it is, as stated, greatly diminished. In the former generations substantially all the people contributed to the construction of the highways under the statute labor system, but at the present time not more than half the population is subject to this service, and this, too, at a time when the need for highway improvement is greatest.

While the former ways and means are inadequate or inapplicable to present needs and conditions, there are other means more suitable for the service, and existing in ample proportion for every need. The tollgate-keeper cannot be called upon to restore the ancient system of turnpikes and plank roads to be maintained by a tax upon vehicles passing over them, but there can be provided a general fund in each county sufficient to build up free roads better than the toll roads and with a smaller burden of cost upon the people. The statute labor in the rural districts cannot be depended upon, because it is unsuitable to the service now required and spasmodic in its application, when it should be perennial; but this statute labor can be commuted to a money tax, with no hardships upon the citizens and with great benefit to the highway system.

Former inhabitants of the abandoned farms or the deserted villages cannot be followed to the great cities and the road tax which they formerly paid be collected from them again to improve the country roads; but it can be provided that all the property owners in every city, as well as in every county, shall pay a money tax into a general fund, which shall be devoted exclusively to the improvement of highways in the rural districts. The state itself can maintain a general fund out of which a portion of the cost of every principal highway in the state shall be paid, and by so doing all the people of the state will contribute to improving the highways, as they once did in the early history of the nation, when substantially all the wealth and population was distributed almost equally throughout the settled portions of the country.

Having a general fund of money instead of statute labor, it would be possible to introduce more scientific and more economical methods of construction with coöperation. This coöperation, formerly applied with good results to the primitive conditions, but which has been partially lost by the diminution in the number and skill of the co-workers, would be restored again in a great measure by drawing the money with which to improve the roads out of a general fund to which all had contributed.

In many countries the army has been used to advantage in time of peace in building up and maintaining the highways. There is no army in this country for such a purpose, but there is an army of prisoners in every state, whose labor is so directed, and has been so directed for generations past, that it adds little or nothing to the common wealth. The labor of these prisoners, properly applied and directed, would be of great benefit and improvement to the highways, and would add greatly to the national wealth, while at the same time it would lighten the pressure of competition with free labor by withdrawing the prison labor from the manufacture of commercial articles and applying it to work not now performed, that is, the building of highways or preparing material to be used therefor.

The General Government, having withdrawn from the field of road construction in 1832, has since done little in that line until very recently. Eight years ago Congress appropriated a small sum of money for the purpose of instituting a sort of inquiry into the prevailing condition of things pertaining to road matters. This appropriation has been continued from year to year and increased during the last two years with a view of coöperating to a limited extent with other efforts in road construction.

The General Government can perform certain duties pertaining to scientific road improvement better than any other agency. Scientific facts ascertained at one time by the General Government will serve for the enlightenment of the people of all the states, and with no more cost than would be required for each single state to make the investigation and ascertain the facts for itself.

With a view to securing scientific facts in reference to the value of road-building materials, the Secretary of Agriculture has established at Washington, D. C., a mechanical and chemical laboratory for testing such material from all parts of the country. Professor L. W. Page, late of Harvard University, is in charge of this laboratory, and has tested many samples of rock without charge to those having the test made. There is, however, no test equal to the actual application of the material to the road itself.

With a view to making more extensive tests than could be done by laboratory work alone, the Director of the Office of Public Road Inquiries has, during the past two years, coöperated with the local authorities in many different states in building short sections of object-lesson roads. In this work it is intended not only to contribute something by way of coöperation on the part of the General Government, but also to secure coöperation on the part of as many different interests connected with the road question as possible. The local community having the road built is most largely interested, and is expected to furnish the common labor and domestic material. The railroad companies generally coöperate, because they are interested in having better roads to and from their railroad stations. They therefore contribute by transporting free or at very low rates the machinery and such foreign material as is needed in the construction of the road. The manufacturers of earth-handling and road-building machinery coöperate by furnishing all needed machinery for the most economical construction of the road, and in many cases prison labor is used in preparing material which finally goes into the completed roadbed. The contribution which the General Government makes in this scheme of coöperation is both actually and relatively small, but it is by means of this limited coöperation that it has been possible to produce a large number of object-lesson roads in different states. These have proved very beneficial, not only in showing the scientific side of the question, but the economical side as well.

In the year 1900 object-lesson roads were built under the direction of the Office of Public Road Inquiries near Port Huron, Saginaw, and Traverse City, Michigan; Springfield, Illinois; and Topeka, Kansas. Since that time the object-lesson roads so built have been extended and duplicated by the local authorities without further aid from the government. The people are so well pleased with the results of these experiments that they are making preparations for additional extensions, aggregating many miles.

During the year 1901 sample object-lesson roads were built on a larger scale in coöperation with the Illinois Central, Lake Shore, and Southern railroad companies, and the National Association for Good Roads in the states of Louisiana, Mississippi, Tennessee, Kentucky, Illinois, New York, North Carolina, South Carolina, Alabama, and Georgia. In all of these cases the coöperation has been very hearty on the part of the state, the county, and the municipality in which the work has been done, and the results have been very satisfactory and beneficial.

Hon. A. H. Longino, governor of Mississippi, in his speech made at the International Good Roads Congress at Buffalo, September 17, 1901, said:

> "My friends, the importance of good roads seems to me to be so apparent, so self-evident, that the discussion thereof is but a discussion of truisms. Much as we appreciate railroads, rivers, and canals as means for transportation of the commerce of the country, they are, in my judgment, of less importance to mankind, to the masses of the people, and to all classes of people, than are good country roads.
>
> "I live in a section of the country where that important subject has found at the hands of the people apparently less appreciation and less effort toward improvement than in many others. In behalf of the Good Roads Association, headed by Colonel Moore and Mr. Richardson, which recently met in the state of Mississippi, I want to say that more interest has been aroused by their efforts concerning this important subject among the people there than perhaps ever existed before in the history of the state. By their work, demonstrating what could be done by the methods which they employed, and by their agitation of the question, the people have become aroused as they never were before; and since their departure from the state a large number of counties which were not already working under the contract system have provided for public highways, worked by contract, requiring the contractor to give a good and sufficient bond, a bond broad enough in its provisions and large enough in amount to compel faithful service;

and Mississippi is today starting out on a higher plane than ever before."

FOOTNOTE:

[5] By Hon. Martin Dodge, Director of the Office of Public Road Inquiries.

CHAPTER III
GOOD ROADS FOR FARMERS[6]

Poor roads constitute the greatest drawback to rural life, and for the lack of good roads the farmers suffer more than any other class. It is obviously unnecessary, therefore, to discuss here the benefits to be derived by them from improved roads. Suffice it to say, that those localities where good roads have been built are becoming richer, more prosperous, and more thickly settled, while those which do not possess these advantages in transportation are either at a standstill or are becoming poorer and more sparsely settled. If these conditions continue, fruitful farms may be abandoned and rich lands go to waste. Life on a farm often becomes, as a result of "bottomless roads," isolated and barren of social enjoyments and pleasures, and country people in some communities suffer such great disadvantage that ambition is checked, energy weakened, and industry paralyzed.

Good roads, like good streets, make habitation along them most desirable; they economize time and force in transportation of products, reduce wear and tear on horses, harness and vehicles, and enhance the market value of real estate. They raise the value of farm lands and farm products, and tend to beautify the country through which they pass; they facilitate rural mail delivery and are a potent aid to education, religion, and sociability. Charles Sumner once said: "The road and the schoolmaster are the two most important agents in advancing civilization."

TYPICAL MACADAM ROAD NEAR BRYN MAWR,
PENNSYLVANIA

The difference between good and bad roads is often equivalent to the difference between profit and loss. Good roads have a money value to farmers as well as a political and social value, and leaving out convenience, comfort, social and refined influences which good roads always enhance, and looking at them only from the "almighty dollar" side, they are found to pay handsome dividends each year.

People generally are beginning to realize that road-building is a public matter, and that the best interests of American agriculture and the American people as a whole demand the construction of good roads, and that money wisely expended for this purpose is sure to return.

Road-making is perfected by practice, experience, and labor. Soils and clays, sand and ores, gravels and rocks, are transformed into beautiful roads, streets, and boulevards, by methods which conform with their great varieties of characters and with nature's laws. The art of road-building depends largely for its success upon being carried on in conformity with certain general principles.

It is necessary that roads should be hard, smooth, comparatively level, and fit for use at all seasons of the year; that they should be properly located, or laid out on the ground, so that their grades may be such that animate or inanimate power may be applied upon them to the best advantage and without great loss of energy; that they should be properly constructed, the ground well drained, the roadbed graded, shaped, and rolled, and that they should be surfaced with the best material procurable; that they should be properly maintained or kept constantly in good repair.

All the important roads in the United States can be and doubtless will be macadamized or otherwise improved in the not distant future. This expectation should govern their present location and treatment everywhere. Unless changes are made in the location of the roads in many parts of this country it would be worse than folly to macadamize them. "Any costly resurfacing of the existing roads will fasten them where they are for generations," says General Stone. The chief difficulty in this country is not with the surface, but with the steep grades, many of which are too long to be reduced by cutting and filling on the present lines, and if this could be done it would cost more in many cases than relocating them.

Many of our roads were originally laid out without any attention to general topography, and in most cases followed the settler's path from cabin to cabin, the pig trail, or ran along the boundary lines of the farms regardless of grades or direction. Most of them remain today where they were located years ago, and where untold labor, expense, and energy have been wasted in trying to haul over them and in endeavors to improve their deplorable condition.

The great error is made of continuing to follow these primitive paths with our public highways. The right course is to call in an engineer and throw the road around the end or along the side of steep hills instead of continuing to go over them, or to pull the road up on dry solid ground instead of splashing through the mud and water of the creek or swamp. Far more time and money have been wasted in trying to keep up a single mile of one of these "pig-track" surveys than it would take to build and keep in repair two miles of good road.

Another and perhaps greater error is made by some persons in the West who continue to lay out their roads on "section lines." These sections are all square, with sides running north, south, east, and west. A person wishing to cross the country in any other than these directions must necessarily do so in rectangular zigzags. It also necessitates very often the crossing and recrossing of hills and valleys, which might be avoided if the roads had been constructed on scientific principles.

A STUDY IN GRADING

[The old road had a grade of eight per cent; by the improved route the grade is four per cent]

In the prairie state of Iowa, for example, where roads are no worse than in many other states, there is a greater number of roads having much steeper grades than are found in the mountainous republic of Switzerland. In Maryland the old stagecoach road or turnpike running from Washington to Baltimore makes almost a "bee line," regardless of hills or valleys, and the grades at places are as steep as ten or twelve per cent, where by making little detours the road might have been made perfectly level, or by running it up the hills less abruptly the grade might have been reduced to three or four per cent, as is done in the hilly regions of many parts of this and other countries. Straight roads are the proper kind to have, but in hilly countries their straightness should always be sacrificed to obtain a level surface so as to better accommodate the people who use them.

Graceful and natural curves conforming to the lay of the land add beauty to the landscape, besides enhancing the value of property. Not only do level, curved roads add beauty to the landscape and make lands along them more valuable, but the horse is able to utilize his full strength over them; furthermore, a horse can pull only four-fifths as much on a grade of two feet in one hundred feet, and this gradually lessens until with a grade of ten feet in one hundred feet he can draw but one-fourth as much as he can on a level road.

All roads should therefore wind around hills or be cut through instead of running over them, and in many cases the former can be done without greatly increasing the distance. To illustrate, if an apple or pear be cut in half and one of the halves placed on a flat surface, it will be seen that the horizontal distance around from stem to blossom is no greater than the distance over between the same points.

The wilfulness of one or two private individuals sometimes becomes a barrier to traffic and commerce. The great drawback to the laying out of roads on the principle referred to is that of the necessity, in some cases, of building them through the best lands, the choicest pastures and orchards, instead, as they do now, of cutting around the farm line or passing through old worn-out fields or over rocky knolls. But if farmers wish people to know that they have good farms, good cattle, sheep, or horses, good grain, fruit, or vegetables, they should let the roads go through the best parts of the farms.

The difference in length between a straight road and one which is slightly curved is less than one would imagine. Says Sganzin: "If a road between two places ten miles apart were made to curve so that the eye could see no farther than a quarter of a mile of it at once, its length would exceed that of a perfectly straight road between the same points by only about one hundred and fifty yards." Even if the distance around a hill be much greater, it is often more economical to construct it that way than to go over and necessitate the expenditure of large amounts of money in reducing the grade, or a waste of much valuable time and energy in transporting goods that way. Gillespie says "that, as a general rule, the horizontal length of a road may be advantageously increased to avoid an ascent by at least twenty times the perpendicular height which is thus to be avoided—that is, to escape a hill one hundred feet high it would be proper for the road to make such a circuit as would increase its length two thousand feet." The mathematical axiom that "a straight line is the shortest distance between two points" is not, therefore, the best rule to follow in laying out a road; better is the proverb that "the longest way round is the shortest way home."

The grade is the most important factor to be considered in the location of roads. The smoother the road surface, the less the grade should be.

Whether the road be constructed of earth, stone, or gravel, steep grades should always be avoided if possible. They become covered at times with coatings of ice or slippery soil, making them very difficult to ascend with loaded vehicles, as well as dangerous to descend. They allow water to rush down at such a rate as to wash great gaps alongside or to carry the surfacing material away. As the grade increases in steepness either the load has to be diminished in proportion or more horses or power attached. From Gillespie we find that if a horse can draw on a level one thousand pounds, on a rise of —

1 foot in—	Pounds
100 feet he draws	900
50 feet	810
44 feet	750
40 feet	720
30 feet	640
25 feet	540
24feet	500
20 feet	400
10 feet	250

It is therefore seen that when the grades are 1 foot in 44 feet, or 120 feet to the mile, a horse can draw only three-fourths as much as he can on a level; where the grade is 1 foot in 24 feet, or 220 feet to the mile, he can draw only one-half as much, and on a ten per cent grade, or 520 feet to the mile, he is able to draw only one-fourth as much as on a level road.

As a chain is no stronger than its weakest link, just so the greatest load which can be hauled over a road is the load which can be hauled through the deepest mud hole or up the steepest hill on that road. The cost of haulage is, therefore, necessarily increased in proportion to the roughness of the surface or steepness of the grade. It costs one and one-half times as much to haul over a road having a five per cent grade and three times as much over one having a ten per cent grade as on a level road. As a perfectly level road can seldom be had, it is well to know the steepest allowable grade. If the hill be one of great length, it is sometimes best to have the lowest part steepest, upon which the horse is capable of exerting his full strength, and to make the slope more gentle toward the summit, to correspond with the continually decreasing strength of the fatigued animal.

So far as descent is concerned, a road should not be so steep that the wagons and carriages cannot be drawn down it with perfect ease and safety. Sir Henry Parnell considered that when the grade was no greater than one foot in thirty-five feet, vehicles could be drawn down it at a speed of twelve miles an hour with perfect safety. Gillespie says:

"It has been ascertained that a horse can for a short time double his usual exertion; also, that on the best roads he exerts a pressure against his collar of about one thirty-fifth of the load. If he can double his exertion for a time, he can pull one thirty-fifth more, and the slope which would force him to lift that proportion would be, as seen from the above table, one of one in thirty-five, or about a three per cent grade. On this slope, however, he would be compelled to double his ordinary exertion to draw a full load, and it would therefore be the maximum grade." Mr. Isaac B. Potter, an eminent authority upon roads, says:

"Dirty water and watery dirt make bad going, and mud is the greatest obstacle to the travel and traffic of the farmer. Mud is a mixture of dirt and water. The dirt is always to be found in the roadway, and the water, which comes in rain, snow, and frost, softens it; horses and wagons and narrow wheel tires knead it and mix it, and it soon gets into so bad a condition that a fairly loaded wagon cannot be hauled through it.

"We cannot prevent the coming of this water, and it only remains for us to get rid of it, which can be speedily done if we go about it in the right way. Very few people know how great an amount of water falls upon the country road, and it may surprise some of us to be told that on each mile of an ordinary country highway three rods wide within the United States there falls each year an average of twenty-seven thousand tons of water. In the ordinary country dirt road the water seems to stick and stay as if there was no other place for it, and this is only because we have never given it a fair opportunity to run out of the dirt and find its level in other places. We cannot make a hard road out of soft mud, and no amount of labor and machinery will make a good dirt road that will stay good unless some plan is adopted to get rid of the surplus water. Water is a heavy, limpid fluid, hard to confine and easy to let loose. It is always seeking for a chance to run down a hill; always trying to find its lowest level."

An essential feature of a good road is good drainage, and the principles of good drainage remain substantially the same whether the road be constructed of earth, gravel, shells, stones, or asphalt. The first demand of good drainage is to attend to the shape of road surface. This must be "crowned," or rounded up toward the center, so that there may be a fall from the center to the sides, thus compelling the water to flow rapidly from the surface into the gutters which should be constructed on one or both sides, and from there in turn be discharged into larger and more open channels. Furthermore, it is necessary that no water be allowed to flow across a roadway; culverts, tile, stone, or box drains should be provided for that purpose.

In addition to being well covered and drained, the surface should be kept as smooth as possible; that is, free from ruts, wheel tracks, holes, or hollows. If any of these exist, instead of being thrown to the side the water is held back and is either evaporated by the sun or absorbed by the material of which the road is constructed. In the latter case the material loses its solidity, softens and yields to the impact of the horses' feet and the wheels of vehicles, and, like the water poured upon a grindstone, so the water poured on a road surface which is not properly drained assists the grinding action of the wheels in rutting or completely destroying the surface. When water is allowed to stand on a road the holes and ruts rapidly increase in number and size; wagon after wagon sinks deeper and deeper, until the road finally becomes utterly bad, and sometimes impassable, as frequently found in many parts of the country during the winter season.

Road drainage is just as essential to a good road as farm drainage is to a good farm. In fact, the two go hand in hand, and the better the one the better the other, and vice versa. There are thousands of miles of public roads in the United States which are practically impassable during some portion of the year on account of bad drainage, while for the same reason thousands of acres of the richest meadow and swamp lands lie idle from year in to year out.

The wearing surface of a road must be in effect a roof; that is, the section in the middle should be the highest part and the traveled roadway should be made as impervious to water as possible, so that it will flow freely and quickly into the gutters or ditches alongside. The best shape for the cross section of a road has been found to be either a flat ellipse or one made up of two plane surfaces sloping uniformly from the middle to the sides and joined in the center by a small, circular curve. Either of these sections may be used, provided it is not too flat in the middle for good drainage or too steep at the gutters for safety. The steepness of the slope from the center to the sides should depend upon the nature of the surface, being greater or less according to its roughness or smoothness. This slope ought to be greatest on earth roads, perhaps as much in some cases as one foot in twenty feet after the surface has been thoroughly rolled or compacted by traffic. This varies from about one in twenty to one in thirty on a macadam road, to one in forty or one in sixty on the various classes of pavements, and for asphalt sometimes as low as one in eighty.

Where the road is constructed on a grade or hill the slope from the center to the sides should be slightly steeper than that on the level road. The best cross section for roads on grades is the one made up from two plane surfaces sloping uniformly from the center to the sides. This is done so as to avoid the danger of overturning near the side ditches, which would necessarily be increased if the elliptical form were used. The slope from the center to the sides must be steep enough to lead the water into the side ditches instead of allowing it to run down the middle of the road. Every wheel track on an inclined roadway becomes a channel for carrying down the water, and unless the curvature is sufficient these tracks are quickly deepened into water courses which cut into and sometimes destroy the best improved road.

In order to prevent the washing out of earth roads on hills it sometimes becomes necessary to construct water breaks; that is, broad shallow ditches arranged so as to catch the surface water and carry it each way into the side ditches. Such ditches retard traffic to a certain extent, and often result in overturning vehicles; consequently they should never be used until all other means have failed to cause the water to flow into the side channels; neither should they be allowed to cross the entire width of the road diagonally, but should be constructed in the shape of the letter V. This arrangement permits teams following the middle of the road to cross the ditch squarely and thus avoid the danger of overturning. These ditches should not be deeper than is absolutely necessary to throw the water off the surface, and the part in the center should be the shallowest.

Unfortunately farmers and road masters have a fixed idea that one way to prevent hills, long and short, from washing is to heap upon them quantities of those original tumular obstructions known indifferently as "thank-you-ma'ams," "breaks," or "hummocks," and the number they can squeeze in upon a single hill is positively astonishing. Quoting Mr. Isaac B. Potter:

> "Side ditches are necessary because the thousands of tons of water which fall upon every mile of country road each year, in the form of rain or snow, should be carried away to some neighboring creek or other water channel as fast as the rain falls and the snow melts, so as to prevent its forming mud and destroying the surface of the road. When the ground is frozen and a heavy rain or sudden thaw occurs, the side ditch is the only means of getting rid of the surface water; for no matter how sandy or porous the soil may be, when filled with frost it is practically water-tight, and the water which falls or forms on the surface must either remain there or be carried away by surface ditches at the sides of the road.

> "A side ditch should have a gradually falling and even grade at the bottom, and broad, flaring sides to prevent the caving in of its banks. It can be easily cleared of snow, weeds, and rubbish; the water will

run into it easily from each side, and it is not dangerous to wagons and foot travelers. It is therefore a much better ditch than the kind of ditch very often dug by erosion along the country roadside."

Where the road is built on a grade some provision should be made to prevent the wash of the gutters into great, deep gullies. This can be done by paving the bottom and sides of the gutters with brick, river rocks, or field stone. In order to make the flow in such side ditches as small as possible it is advisable to construct outlets into the adjacent fields or to lay underground pipes or tile drains with openings into the ditches at frequent intervals.

The size of side ditches should depend upon the character of the soil and the amount of water they are expected to carry. If possible they should be located three feet from the edge of the traveled roadway, so that if the latter is fourteen feet wide there will be twenty feet of clear space between ditches.

The bottom of the ditch may vary in width from three to twelve inches, or even more, as may be found necessary in order to carry the largest amount of water which is expected to flow through it at any one time. Sometimes the only ditches necessary to carry off the surface water are those made by the use of the road machines or road graders. The blade of the machine may be set at any desired angle, and when drawn along by horses, cuts into the surface and moves the earth from the sides toward the center, forming gutters alongside and distributing the earth uniformly over the traveled way. Such gutters are liable to become clogged by brush, weeds, and other débris, or destroyed by passing wagons, and it is therefore better, when the space permits, to have the side ditches above referred to, even if the road be built with a road machine.

In order to have a good road it is just as necessary that water should not be allowed to attack the substructure from below as that it should not be permitted to percolate through it from above. Especially is the former provision essential in cold climates, where, if water is allowed to remain in the substructure, the whole roadway is liable to become broken up and destroyed by frost and the wheels of vehicles. Therefore, where the road runs through low wet lands or over certain kinds of clayey soils, surface drainage is not all that is necessary. Common side drains catch surface water and surface water only. Isaac Potter says:

"Many miles of road are on low, flat lands and on springy soils, and thousands of miles of prairie roads are, for many weeks in the year, laid on a wet subsoil. In all such cases, and, indeed, in every case where the nature of the ground is not such as to insure quick drainage, the road may be vastly benefited by under drainage. An under drain clears the soil of surplus water, dries it, warms it, and makes impossible the formation of deep, heavy, frozen crusts, which are found in every undrained road when the severe winter weather follows the heavy fall rains. This crust causes nine-tenths of the difficulties of travel in the time of sudden or long-continued thaws.

"Roads constructed over wet undrained lands are always difficult to manage and expensive to maintain, and they are liable to be broken up in wet weather or after frosts. It will be much cheaper in the long run to go to the expense of making the drainage of the subjacent soil and substructure as perfect as possible. There is scarcely an earth road in the United States which cannot be so improved by surface or subdrainage as to yield benefits to the farmers a hundred times greater in value than the cost of the drains themselves.

"Under drains are not expensive. On the contrary, they are cheap and easily made, and if made in a substantial way and according to the rules of common sense a good under drain will last for ages. Use the best tools and materials you can get; employ them as well as you know how, and wait results with a clear conscience. Slim fagots of wood bound together and laid lengthwise at the bottom of a carefully graded drain ditch will answer fairly well if stone or drain tile cannot be had, and will be of infinite benefit to a dirt road laid on springy soils."

Subdrains should be carefully graded with a level at the bottom to a depth of about four feet, and should have a continuous fall throughout their entire length of at least six inches for each one hundred feet in length. If tile drains cannot be had, large, flat stones may be carefully placed so as to form a clear, open passage at the bottom for the flow of the water. The ditch should then be half filled with rough field stones, and on these a layer of smaller stones or gravel and a layer of sod, hay, gravel, cinders, or straw, or, if none of these can be had, of soil. If field stones or drain tile cannot be procured, satisfactory results may be attained by the use of logs and brush.

If there be springs in the soil which might destroy the stability of the road, they should, if possible, be tapped and the water carried under or along the side until it can be turned away into some side channel. Such drains may be made of bundles of brush, field stones, brick, or drain tiles. They should be so protected by straw, sod, or brush as to prevent the soil from washing in and clogging them.

Most of the roads in this country are of necessity constructed of earth, while in a few of the richer and more enterprising communities the most important thoroughfares are surfaced with gravel, shell, stones, or other materials. Unless some new system for the improvement of public roads is adopted, the inability of rural communities to raise funds for this purpose will necessarily cause the construction of hard roads to be very gradual for some time to come. Until this new system is adopted the most important problem will be that of making the most of the roads which exist, rather than building new ones of specially prepared materials. The natural materials and the funds already available must be used with skill and judgment in order to secure the best results. The location, grades, and drainage having been treated in the preceding pages, the next and most important consideration is that of constructing and improving the various kinds of roads.

Of earth roads, as commonly built, it suffices to say that their present conditions should not be tolerated in communities where there are any other materials with which to improve them. Earth is the poorest of all road materials, aside from sand, and earth roads require more attention than any other kind of roads, and as a rule get less. At best, they possess so many defects that they should have all the attention and care of which their condition is susceptible. With earth alone, however, a very passable road can be made, provided the principles of location, drainage, and shape of surface, together with that of keeping the surface as smooth and firm as possible by rolling, be strictly adhered to. In fact a good earth road is second to none for summer travel and superior to many of the so-called macadam or stone roads.

"Water is the great road destroyer," and too much attention cannot be given to the surface and subdrainage of earth roads. The material of which their surfaces are composed is more susceptible to the action of water and more easily destroyed by it than any other highway material. Drainage alone will often change a bad road into a good one, while on the other hand the best road may be destroyed by the absence of good drains.

The same can be said of rolling, which is a very important matter in attempting to build or maintain a satisfactory earth road. If loose earth is dumped into the middle of the road and consolidated by traffic, the action of the narrow-tired wheels cuts it or rolls it into uneven ruts and ridges, which hold water, and ultimately results, if in the winter season, in a sticky, muddy surface, or if it be in dry weather, in covering the surface with several inches of dust. If, however, the surface be prepared with a road machine and properly rolled with a heavy roller, it can usually be made sufficiently firm and smooth to sustain the traffic without rutting, and resist the penetrating action of the water. Every road is made smoother, harder, and better by rolling. Such rolling should be done in damp weather, or if that is not possible, the surface should be sprinkled if the character of the soil requires such aid for its proper consolidation.

In constructing new earth roads all stumps, brush, vegetable matter, rocks, and bowlders should be removed from the surface and the resulting holes filled in with suitable material, carefully and thoroughly tamped or rolled, before the road embankment is commenced. No perishable material should be used in forming the permanent embankments. Where possible the longitudinal grade should be kept down to one foot in thirty feet, and should under no circumstances exceed one in twenty, while that from center to sides should be maintained at one foot in twenty feet.

Wherever the subgrade soil is found unsuitable it should be removed and replaced with good material rolled to a bearing, *i.e.*, so as to be smooth and compact. The roadbed, having been brought to the required grade and crown, should be rolled several times to compact the surface. All inequalities discovered during the rolling should be leveled up and rerolled. On the prepared subgrade, the earth should be spread, harrowed if necessary, and then rolled to a bearing by passing the unballasted road roller a number of times over every portion of the surface of the section.

In level countries and with narrow roads, enough material may be excavated to raise the roadway above the subgrade in forming the side ditches by means of road machines. If not, the required earth should be obtained by widening the side excavations, or from cuttings on the line of the new roadway, or from pits close by, elevating graders and modern dumping or spreading wagons being preferably used for this purpose. When the earth is brought up to the final height, it is again harrowed, then trimmed by means of road levelers or road machines and ultimately rolled to a solid and smooth surface with road rollers gradually increased in weight by the addition of ballast.

No filling should be brought up in layers exceeding nine inches in depth. During the rolling, sprinkling should be attended to wherever the character of the soil requires such aid. The cross section of the roadway must be maintained during the last rolling stage by the addition of earth as needed. On clay soils a layer of sand, gravel, or ashes spread on the roadway will prevent the sticking of the clay to the roller. As previously explained, the finishing touches to the road surface should be given by a heavy roller.

Before the earth road is opened to traffic, deep and wide side ditches should be constructed, with a fall throughout their entire length of at least one in one hundred and twenty. They should be cleaned and left with the drain tiling connections, if any, in good working order.

Clay soils, as a rule, absorb water quite freely and soften when saturated, but water does not readily pass through them; hence they are not easily subdrained. When used alone, clay is the least desirable of all road materials, but roads constructed over clay soils may be treated with sand or small gravel, from which a comparatively hard and compact mass is formed which is nearly impervious to water. Material of this character found in the natural state, commonly known as hardpan, makes, when properly applied, a very solid and durable surface. In soil composed of a mixture of sand, gravel, and clay, all that is necessary to make a good road of its kind is to "crown" the surface, keep the ruts and hollows filled, and the ditches open and free.

Sand Clay Road in Richland County, South Carolina

[Sand soil with nine inches of clay and two inches cover of sand]

Roads are prone to wear in ruts, and when hollows and ruts begin to make their appearance on the surface of an earth road great care should be used in selecting new material, with which they should be immediately filled, because a hole which could have been filled at first with a shovel full of material would soon need a cart full. It should, if possible, be of a gravelly nature, entirely free from vegetable earth, muck, or mold. Sod or turf should not be placed on the surface, neither should the surface be renewed by throwing upon it the worn-out material from the gutters alongside. The last injunction, if rightly observed and the proper remedy applied, would doubtless put an end to the deplorable condition of thousands of miles of earth roads in the United States.

A road-maker should not go to the other extreme and fill up ruts and holes with stone or large gravel. In many cases it would be wiser to dump such material in the river. These stones do not wear uniformly with the rest of the material, but produce bumps and ridges, and in nearly every case result in making two holes instead of one. Every hole or rut in a roadway, if not tamped full of some good material like that of which the road is constructed, will become filled with water, and finally with mud and water, and will be dug deeper and wider by each passing vehicle.

The work of maintaining earth roads will be much increased by lack of care in properly finishing the work. The labor and money spent in rolling a newly-made road may save many times that amount of labor and money in making future repairs. After the material has been placed it should not be left for the traffic to consolidate, or for the rains to wash off into the ditches, but should be carefully formed and surfaced, and then, if possible, rolled. The rolling not only consolidates the material, but puts the roadbed in proper shape for travel immediately. If there is anything more trying on man or beast than to travel over an unimproved road, it must be to travel over one which has just been "worked" by the antiquated methods now in vogue in many of the states.

The traveled way should never be repaired by the use of plows or scoops. The plow breaks up the compact surface which age and traffic have made tolerable. Earth roads can be rapidly repaired by a judicious use of road machines and road rollers. The road machine places the material where it is most needed, and the roller compacts and keeps it there. The labor-saving machinery now manufactured for road-building is just as effectual and necessary as the modern mower, self-binder, and thrasher. Road graders and rollers are the modern inventions necessary to permanent and economical construction. Two men with two teams can build more road in one day with a grader and roller than fifty men can with picks and shovels, and do it more uniformly and more thoroughly.

Doubtless the best way to keep an earth road, or any road, for that matter, in repair is by the use of wide tires on all wagons carrying heavy burdens. Water and narrow tires aid each other in destroying streets, macadam, gravel, and earth roads. Narrow tires are also among the most destructive agents to the fields, pastures, and meadows of farms, while on the other hand wide tires are road-makers; they roll and harden the surface, and every loaded wagon becomes in effect a road roller. Nothing so much tends to the improving of a road as the continued rolling of its surface.

Tests recently made at the experiment stations in Utah and Missouri show that wide tires not only improve the surface of roads, but that under ordinary circumstances less power is required to pull a wagon on which wide tires are used. The introduction in recent years of a wide metallic tire which can be placed on any narrow-tired wheel at the cost of two dollars each, has removed one very serious objection to the proposed substitution of broad tires for the narrow ones now in use.

Repairs on earth roads should be attended to particularly in the spring of the year, but the great mistake of letting all the repairs go until that time should rot be made. The great want of the country road is daily care, and the sooner we do away with the system of "working out" our road taxes, and pay such taxes in money, the sooner will it be possible to build improved roads and to hire experts to keep them constantly in good repair. Roads could then secure attention when such attention is most needed. If they are repaired only annually or semiannually they are seldom in good condition but when they are given daily or weekly care they are almost always in good condition, and, moreover, the second method costs far less than the first. A portion of all levy tax money raised for road purposes should be used in buying improved road machinery, and in constructing each year a few miles of improved stone or gravel roads.

The only exceptions to the instructions given on road drainage are found in the attempt to improve a sand road. The more one improves the drainage of a sand road the more deplorable becomes its condition. Nothing will ruin one quicker than to dig a ditch on each side and drain all the water away. The best way to make such a road firm is to keep it constantly damp. Very bushy or shady trees alongside such roads prevent the evaporation of water.

The usual way of mending roads which run over loose sandy soils is to cover the surface with tough clay or mix the clay and sand together. This is quite an expensive treatment if the clay has to be transported a great distance, but the expense may be reduced by improving only eight or ten feet or half of the roadway.

Any strong, fibrous substance, and especially one which holds moisture, such as the refuse of sugar cane or sorghum, and even common straw, flax, or swamp grass, will be useful. Spent tan is of some service, and wood fiber in any form is excellent. The best is the fibrous sawdust made in sawing shingles by those machines which cut lengthwise of the fiber into the side of the block. Sawdust is first spread on the road from eight to ten inches deep, and this is covered with sand to protect the road against fire lighted from pipes or cigars carelessly thrown or emptied on the roadbed. The sand also keeps the sawdust damp. The dust and sand soon become hard and packed, and the wheels of the heaviest wagons make but little impression upon the surface. The roadbed appears to be almost as solid as a plank road, but is much easier for the teams. The road prepared in this manner will remain good for four or five years and will then require renewing in some parts. The ordinary lumber sawdust would not be so good, of course, but if mixed with planer shavings might serve fairly well.

Roads built of poles or logs laid across the roadway are called corduroy roads, because of their corrugated or ribbed appearance. Like earth roads, they should never be built where it is possible to secure any other good material; but, as is frequently the case in swampy, timbered regions, other material is unavailable, and as the road would be absolutely impassable without them at certain seasons of the year, it is well to know how to make them. Roads of this character should be fifteen or sixteen feet wide, so as to enable wagons to pass each other. Logs are superior to poles for this purpose and should be used if possible. The following in regard to the construction of corduroy roads is from Gilmore's *Roads, Streets, and Pavements*:

"The logs are all cut the same length, which should be that of the required width of the road, and in laying them down such care in selection should be exercised as will give the smallest joints or openings between them. In order to reduce as much as possible the resistance to draft and the violence of the repeated shocks to which vehicles are subjected upon these roads, and also to render its surface practicable for draft animals, it is customary to level up between the logs with smaller pieces of the same length but split to a triangular cross section. These are inserted with edges downward in the open joints, so as to bring their surface even with the upper sides of the large logs, or as nearly so as practicable.

"Upon the bed thus prepared a layer of brushwood is put, with a few inches in thickness, with soil or turf on top to keep it in place. This completes the road. The logs are laid directly upon the natural surface of the soil, those of the same or nearly of the same diameter being kept together, and the top covering of soil is excavated from side ditches.

"Cross drains may usually be omitted in roads of this kind, as the openings between the logs, even when laid with utmost care, will furnish more than ample water way for drainage from the ditch on the upper to that on the lower side of the road. When the passage of a creek of considerable volume is to be provided for, and in localities subject to freshets, cross drains or culverts are made wherever necessary by the omission of two or more logs, the openings being bridged with planks, split rails, or poles laid transversely to the axis of the road and resting on cross beams notched into the logs on either side."

The essential requirement of a good road is that it should be firm and unyielding at all times and in all kinds of weather, so that its surface may be smooth and impervious to water. Earth roads at best fulfil none of these requirements, unless they be covered with some artificial material. On a well-made gravel road one horse can draw twice as large a load as he can on a well-made earth road. On a hard smooth stone road one horse can pull as much as four horses will on a good earth road. If larger loads can be hauled and better time made on good hard roads than on good earth ones, the area and the number of people benefited are increased in direct proportion to the improvement of their surface. Moreover, it is evident that a farm four or five miles from the market or shipping point located on or near a hard road is virtually nearer the market than one situated only two or three miles away, but located on a soft and yielding road. Hard roads are divided here into three classes—gravel, shell, and stone.

Although it is impracticable, and in many cases impossible, for communities to build good stone roads, a surface of gravel may frequently be used to advantage, giving far better results than could be attained by the use of earth alone. Where beds of good gravel are available this is the simplest, cheapest, and most effective method of improving country roads.

GRAVEL ROAD NEAR SOLDIERS' HOME, DISTRICT OF COLUMBIA

In connection with the building and maintenance of gravel roads the most important matter to consider is that of selecting the proper material. A small proportion of argillaceous sand, clayey, or earthy matter contained in some gravel enables it to pack readily and consolidate under traffic or the road roller. Seaside and river gravel, which is composed usually of rounded, waterworn pebbles, is unfit for surfacing roads. The small stones of which they are composed, having no angular projections or sharp edges, easily move or slide against each other, and will not bind together, and even when mixed with clay may turn freely, causing the whole surface to be loose, like materials in a shaken sieve.

Inferior qualities of gravel can sometimes be used for foundations; but where it becomes necessary to employ such material even for that purpose it is well to mix just enough sandy or clayey loam to bind it firmly together. For the wearing surface or the top layer the pebbles should, if possible, be comparatively clean, hard, angular, and tough, so that they will readily consolidate and will not be easily pulverized by the impact of traffic, into dust and mud. They should be coarse, varying in size from half an inch to an inch and one-half.

Where blue gravel or hardpan and clean bank gravel are procurable, a good road may be made by mixing the two together. Pit gravel or gravel dug from the earth as a rule contains too much earthy matter. This may, however, be removed by sifting. For this purpose two sieves are necessary, through which the gravel should be thrown. The meshes of one sieve should be one and one-half or two inches in diameter, while the meshes of the other should be three-fourths of an inch. All pebbles which will not go through the one and one-half inch meshes should be rejected or broken so that they will go through. All material which sifts through the three-fourths inch meshes should be rejected for the road, but may be used in making side paths. The excellent road which can be built from materials prepared in this way is so far superior to the one made of the natural clayey material that the expense and trouble of sifting is many times repaid.

The best gravel for road-building stands perpendicular in the bank; that is, when the pit has been opened up the remainder stands compact and firm and cannot be dislodged except by use of the pick, and when it gives way falls in great chunks or solid masses. Such material usually contains tough angular gravel with just enough cementing properties to enable it to readily pack and consolidate, and requires no further treatment than to place it properly on the prepared roadbed.

Some earth roads may be greatly improved by covering the surface with a layer of three or four inches of gravel, and sometimes even a thinner layer may prove of very great benefit if kept in proper repair. The subsoil of such roadway ought, however, to be well drained, or of a light and porous nature. Roads constructed over clay soils require a layer of at least six inches of gravel. The gravel must be deep enough to prevent the weight of traffic forcing the surface material into weak places in the clay beneath, and also to prevent the surface water from percolating through and softening the clay and causing the whole roadway to be torn up.

Owing to a lack of knowledge regarding construction, indifference, or carelessness in building or improving, roads made of gravel are often very much worse than they ought to be. Some of them are made by simply dumping the material into ruts, mud holes, or gutter-like depressions, or on unimproved foundation, and are left thus for traffic to consolidate, while others are made by covering the surface with inferior material without any attention being paid to the fundamental principles of drainage. As a result of such thoughtless and haphazard methods the road usually becomes rougher and more completely covered with holes than before.

In constructing a gravel road the roadbed should first be brought to the proper grade. Ordinarily an excavation is then made to the depth of eight to ten inches, varying in width with the requirements of traffic. For a farm or farming community the width need not be greater than ten or twelve feet. A roadway which is too wide is not only useless, but the extra width is a positive damage. Any width beyond that needed for the traffic is not only a waste of money in constructing the road, but is the cause of a never-ending expense in maintaining it. The surface of the roadbed should preferably have a fall from the center to the sides the same as that to be given the finished road, and should, if possible, be thoroughly rolled and consolidated until perfectly smooth and firm.

A layer, not thicker than four inches, of good gravel, such as that recommended above, should then be spread evenly over the prepared roadbed. Such material is usually carried upon a road in wheelbarrows or dump carts, and then spread in even layers with rakes, but the latest and best device for this purpose is a spreading cart.

If a roller cannot be had, the road is thrown open to traffic until it becomes fairly well consolidated; but it is impossible properly to consolidate materials by the movement of vehicles over the road, and if this means is pursued constant watchfulness is necessary to prevent unequal wear and to keep the surface smooth and free from ruts. The work may be hastened and facilitated by the use of a horse roller or light steam roller; and of course far better results can be accomplished by this means. If the gravel be too dry to consolidate easily it should be kept moist by sprinkling. It should not, however, be made too wet, as any earthy or clayey matter in the gravel is liable to be dissolved.

As soon as the first layer has been properly consolidated, a second, third, and, if necessary, fourth layer, each three or four inches in thickness, is spread on and treated in the same manner, until the road is built up to the required thickness and cross section. The thickness in most cases need not be greater than ten or twelve inches, and the fall from the center to the sides ought not to be greater than one foot in twenty feet, or less than one in twenty-five.

The last or surface layer should be rolled until the wheels of heavily loaded vehicles passing over it make no visible impression. If the top layer is deficient in binding material and will not properly consolidate, a thin layer, not exceeding one inch in thickness, of sand or gravelly loam or clay, should be evenly spread on and slightly sprinkled if in dry weather, before the rolling is begun. Hardpan or stone screenings are much preferred for this purpose if they can be had.

The tendency of material to spread under the roller and work toward the sides can be resisted by rolling that portion nearest the gutters first. To give the surface the required form and to secure uniform density, it is necessary at times to employ men with rakes to fill any depressions which may form.

In order to maintain a gravel road in good condition, it is well to keep piles of gravel alongside at frequent intervals, so that the person who repairs the road can get the material without going too far for it. As soon as ruts or holes appear on the surface some of this good fresh material should be added and tamped into position or kept raked smooth until properly consolidated.

If the surface needs replenishing or rounding up, as is frequently the case with new roads after considerable wear, the material should be applied in sections or patches, raked and rolled until hard and smooth.

Care must be taken that the water from higher places does not drain upon or run across the road. The side ditches, culverts, and drains should be kept open and free from débris.

In many of the Eastern and Southern States road stones do not exist; neither is it possible to secure good coarse gravel. No such material can be secured except at such an expense for freight as to practically preclude its use for road-building. Oyster shells can be secured cheaply in most of these states, and when applied directly upon sand or sandy soil, eight or ten inches in thickness, they form excellent roads for pleasure driving and light traffic. Shells wear much more rapidly than broken stone or gravel of good quality, and consequently roads made of them require more constant attention to keep them in good order. In most cases they should have an entirely new surface every three or four years. When properly maintained they possess many of the qualities found in good stone or gravel roads, and so far as beauty is concerned they cannot be surpassed.

The greatest obstacles to good stone road construction in most places in the United States are the existing methods of building and systems of management, whereby millions of dollars are annually wasted in improper construction or in making trifling repairs on temporary structures.

OYSTER-SHELL OBJECT-LESSON ROAD

[In course of construction, near Mobile, Alabama]

The practice of using too soft, too brittle, or rotten material on roads cannot be too severely condemned. Some people seem to think that if a stone quarries easily, breaks easily, and packs readily, it is the very best stone for road-building. This practice, together with that of placing the material on unimproved foundations and leaving it thus for traffic to consolidate, has done a great deal to destroy the confidence of many people in stone roads. There is no reason in the world why a road should not last for ages if it is built of good material and kept in proper repair. If this is not done, the money spent is more than wasted. It is more economical, as a rule, to bring good materials a long distance by rail or water than to employ inferior ones procured close at hand.

The durability of roads depends largely upon the power of the materials of which they are composed to resist those natural and artificial forces which are constantly acting to destroy them. The fragments of which they are constructed are liable to be attacked in cold climates by frost, and in all climates by water and wind. If composed of stone or gravel, the particles are constantly grinding against each other and being exposed to the impact of the tires of vehicles and the feet of animals. Atmospheric agencies are also at work decomposing and disintegrating the material. It is obviously necessary, therefore, that great care be exercised in selecting for the surfacing of roads those stones which are less liable to be destroyed or decomposed by these physical, dynamical, and chemical forces.

Siliceous materials, those composed of flint or quartz, although hard, are brittle and deficient in toughness. Granite is not desirable because it is composed of three materials of different natures, viz., quartz, feldspar, and mica, the first of which is brittle, the second liable to decompose rapidly, and the third laminable or of a scaly or layerlike nature. Some granites which contain hornblende instead of feldspar are desirable. The darker the variety the better. Gneiss, which is composed of quartz, feldspar, and mica, more or less distinctly slaty, is inferior to granite. Mica-slate stones are altogether useless. The argillaceous slates or clayey slates make a smooth surface, but one which is easily destroyed when wet. The sandstones are utterly useless for road-building. The tougher limestones are very good, but the softer ones, though they bind and make a smooth surface very quickly, are too weak for heavy loads; they wear, wash, and blow away very rapidly.

The materials employed for surfacing roads should be both hard and tough, and should possess by all means cementing and recementing qualities. For the Southern States, where there are no frosts to contend with, the best qualities of limestone are considered quite satisfactory so far as the cementing and recementing qualities are concerned; but in most cases roads of this class of material do not stand the wear and tear of traffic like those built of trap rock, and when exposed to the severe northern winters such material disintegrates very rapidly. In fact, trap rock, "nigger heads," technically known as diabase, and diorites, are considered by most road engineers of long experience to be the very best stones for road-building. Trap rocks as a rule possess all the qualities most desired for road stones. They are hard and tough, and when properly broken to small sizes and rolled thoroughly, cement and consolidate into a smooth, hard crust which is impervious to water, and the broken particles are so heavy that they are not readily broken or washed away.

Unfortunately the most useful stones for road-building are the most difficult to prepare, and as trap rocks are harder to break than any other stones they usually cost more. The foundation or lower courses may be formed of some of the softer stones like gneiss or limestone, but trap rock should be used for the wearing surface, if possible, even if it has to be brought from a distance.

As to the construction of macadam roads, Mr. Potter says:

"In the construction of a macadam road in any given locality, the question of economy generally compels us to use a material found near at hand, and where a local quarry does not exist field stone and stone gathered from the beds of rivers and small streams may often be made to serve every purpose. Many of the stones and boulders thus obtained are of trap rock, and in general it may be said that all hard field and river stones, if broken to a proper size, will make fairly good and sometimes very excellent road metal. No elaborate test is required to determine the hardness of any given specimen. A steel hammer in the hands of an intelligent workman will reveal in a general way the relative degree of toughness of two or more pieces of rock. Field and river stone offer an additional advantage in that they are quickly handled, are generally of convenient size, and are more readily broken either by hand or by machine than most varieties of rock which are quarried in the usual way.

"It is a simple task to break stone for macadam roadways, and by the aid of modern inventions it can be done cheaply and quickly. Hand-broken stone is fairly out of date and is rarely used in America where any considerable amount of work is to be undertaken. Stone may be broken by hand at different points along the roadside where repairs are needed from time to time, but the extra cost of production by this method forbids its being carried on where extended work is undertaken. Hand-broken stone is generally more uniform in size, more nearly cubical in shape, and has sharper angles than that broken by machinery, but the latter, when properly assorted or screened, has been found to meet every requirement.

"A good crusher driven by eight horsepower will turn out from forty to eighty cubic yards of two-inch stone per day of ten hours, and will cost from four hundred dollars upward, according to quality.

"Some crushers are made either stationary, semistationary, or portable, according to the needs of the purchaser, and for country-road work it is sometimes very desirable to have a portable crusher to facilitate its easy transfer from one part of the township to another. The same portable engine that is used in thrashing, sawing wood, and other operations requiring the use of steam power may be used in running a stone crusher, but it is best to remember that a crusher will do its best and most economical work when run by a machine having a horsepower somewhat in excess of the power actually required.

"As the stone comes from the breaker the pieces will be found to show a considerable variety in size, and by many practical road-makers it is regarded as best that these sizes should be assorted and separated, since each has its particular use. To do this work by hand would be troublesome and expensive, and screens are generally employed for that purpose. Screens are not absolutely necessary, and many road-makers do not use them; but they insure uniformity in size of pieces, and uniformity means in many cases superior wear, smoothness, and economy. Most of the screens in common use today are of the rotary kind. In operating they are generally so arranged that the product of the crusher falls directly into the rotary screen, which revolves on an inclined axis and empties the separate pieces into small bins below the crusher. A better form for many purposes includes a larger and more elaborate outfit, in which the stone is carried by an elevator to the screen and by the screen emptied into separate bins according to the respective sizes. From the bins it is easily loaded into wagons or spreading carts and hauled to any desired point along the line of the road.

"The size to which stone should be broken depends upon the quality of the stone, the amount of traffic to which the road will be subjected, and to some extent upon the manner in which the stone is put in place. If a hard, tough stone is employed it may be broken into rough cubes or pieces of about one and a half inches in largest face dimensions, and when broken to such a size the product of the crusher may generally be used to good advantage without the trouble of screening, since dust 'tailings' and fine stuff do not accumulate in large quantities in the breaking of the tougher stone.

"If only moderate traffic is to be provided for, the harder limestones may be broken so the pieces will pass through a two-inch ring, though sizes running from two and a quarter to two and a half inches will insure a more durable roadway, and if a steam roller is used in compacting the metal it will be brought to a smooth surface without much trouble. As a rule, it may be said that to adhere closely to a size running from two and a quarter to two and a half inches in largest face dimensions, and to use care in excluding too large a proportion of small stuff as well as all pieces of excessive size, will insure a satisfactory and durable macadam road."

Macadam insisted that no large stone should ever be employed in road-making, and, indeed, most modern road builders practice his principle that "small angular fragments are the cardinal requirements." As a general rule it has been stated that no stone larger than a walnut should be used for the surfacing of roads.

Stone roads are built in most cases according to the principles laid down by John L. Macadam, while some are built by the methods advocated by Telford. The most important difference between these two principles of construction relates to the propriety or necessity of a paved foundation beneath the crust of broken stone. Telford advocated this principle, while Macadam strongly denied its advantages.

In building roads very few iron-clad rules can be laid down for universal application; skill and judgment must be exercised in designing and building each road so that it will best meet the requirements of the place it is to occupy. The relative value of the telford and macadam systems can most always be determined by the local circumstances, conditions, and necessities under which the road is to be built. The former system seems to have the advantage in swampy, wet places, or where the soil is in strata varying in hardness, or where the foundation is liable to get soft in spots. Under most other circumstances experienced road builders prefer the macadam construction, not only because it is considered best, but also because it is much cheaper.

The macadam road consists of a mass of angular fragments of rock deposited usually in layers upon the roadbed or prepared foundation and consolidated to a smooth, hard surface produced by the passage of vehicles or by use of a road roller. The thickness of this crust varies with the soil, the nature of the stone used, and the amount of traffic which the road is expected to have. It should be so thick that the greatest load will not affect the foundation. The weight usually comes upon a very small part of the surface, but is spread over a large area of the foundation, and the thicker the crust the more uniformly will the load be distributed over the foundation.

Macadam earnestly advocated the principle that all artificial road-building depended wholly for its success upon the making and maintaining of a solid dry foundation and the covering of this foundation with a durable waterproof coating or roof of broken stone. The foundation must be solid and firm; if it be otherwise the crust is useless. A road builder should always remember that without a durable foundation there is no durable road. Hundreds of miles of macadam roads are built in the United States each year on unimproved or unstable foundations and almost as many miles go to pieces for this same reason. Says Macadam:

"The stone is employed to form a secure, smooth, water-tight flooring, over which vehicles may pass with safety and expedition at all seasons of the year. Its thickness should be regulated only by the quality of the material necessary to form such a flooring and not at all by any consideration as to its own independent power of bearing weight…. The erroneous idea that the evils of an underdrained, wet, clayey soil can be remedied by a large quantity of materials has caused a large part of the costly and unsuccessful expenditures in making stone roads."

The evils from improper construction of stone roads are even greater than those resulting from the use of improper material. Macadam never intended that a heterogeneous conglomeration of stones and mud should be called a macadam road. The mistake is often made of depositing broken stone on an old road without first preparing a suitable foundation. The result, in most cases, is that the dirt and mud prevent the stone from packing and by the action of traffic ooze to the surface, while the stones sink deeper and deeper, leaving the road as bad as before.

Another great mistake is often made of spreading large and small stones over a well-graded and well-drained foundation and leaving them thus for traffic to consolidate. The surface of a road left in this manner is often kept in constant turmoil by the larger stones, which work themselves to the surface and are knocked hither and thither by the wheels of vehicles and the feet of animals. These plans of construction cannot be too severelycondemned.

The roadbed should be first graded, then carefully surface-drained. The earth should then be excavated to the depth to which material is to be spread on and the foundation properly shaped and sloped each way from the center so as to discharge any water which may percolate through. This curvature should conform to the curvature of the finished road. A shouldering of firm earth or gravel should be left or made on each side to hold the material in place, and should extend to the gutters at the same curvature as the finished road. The foundation should then be rolled until hard and smooth.

Upon this bed spread a layer of five or six inches of broken stone, which stone should be free from any earthy mixture. This layer should be thoroughly rolled until compact and firm. Stone may be hauled from the stone-crusher bins or from the stone piles in ordinary wheelbarrows or from wagons, and should be distributed broadcast over the surface with shovels, and all inequalities leveled up by the use of rakes. If this method of spreading is employed, grade stakes should be used so as to insure a uniformity of thickness. After the stakes are driven the height of the layer is marked on their sides, and if thought necessary a piece of stout cord is stretched from stake to stake, showing the exact height to which the layer should be spread. Spreading carts have been recently invented which not only place the stone where it is needed without the use of shovels, but spread it on in layers of any desired thickness and at the same time several inches wider than the carts themselves.

If the stones have been separated into two or three different sizes, the largest size should compose the bottom layer, the next size the second layer, etc. The surface of each course or layer should be thoroughly and repeatedly rolled and sprinkled until it becomes firm, compact, and smooth. The first layer, however, should not be sprinkled, as the water is liable to soften the foundation. The rolling ought to be done along the side lines first, gradually working toward the center as the job is being completed. In rolling the last course it is well to begin by rolling first the shoulderings or the side roads if such exist.

A coat of three-quarter inch stone and screenings, of sufficient thickness to make a smooth and uniform surface, should compose the last course, and, like the other layers, should be rolled until perfectly firm and smooth. As a final test of perfection, a small stone placed on the surface will be crushed before being driven into the material.

If none of the stones used be larger than will pass through a two-inch ring, they can be spread on in layers as above described without separating them by screens. Water and binding material—stone screenings or good packing gravel—can be added if found necessary for proper consolidation. Earth or clay should never be used for a binding material. Enough water should be sprinkled on to wash in and fill all voids between the broken stones with binding material and to leave such material damp enough to insure a set.

If a road is built of tough, hard stone, and if the binding material has the same characteristics, a steam roller is essential for speedy results. A horse roller may be used to good advantage if the softer varieties of stone are employed. For general purposes a roller weighing from eight to twelve tons is all that is necessary. Heavier weights are difficult to handle upon unimproved surfaces unless they be constructed like the Addison roller, the weight of which can be increased or lightened at will by filling the drum with water or drawing the water out. This roller can be made to weigh as much as eight tons and, like several other very excellent ones now on the market, is provided with anti-friction roller bearings, which lighten the draft considerably.

Every stone road, unless properly built with small stones and just enough binding material to fill the voids, presents a honeycombed appearance. In fact, a measure containing two cubic feet of broken stone will hold in addition one cubic foot of water, and a cubic yard of broken macadam will weigh just about one-half as much as a solid cubic yard of the same kind of stone. Isaac Potter says:

"To insure a solid roadway and to fill the large proportion of voids or interstices between the different pieces of broken stone, some finer material must be introduced into the structure of the roadway, and this material is usually called a binder, or by some road-makers a 'filler.'

"There used to be much contention regarding the use of binding material in the making of a macadam road, but it is now conceded by nearly all practical and experienced road-makers, both in Europe and America, that the use of a binding material is essential to the proper construction of a good macadam road. It adds to its solidity, insures tightness by closing all of the spaces between the loose, irregular stones, and binds together the macadam crust in a way that gives it firmness, elasticity, and durability."

Binding material to produce the best results should be equal in hardness and toughness with the road stone; the best results are therefore obtained by using screenings or spalls from the broken stone used. Coarse sand and gravel can sometimes be used with impunity as a binder, but the wisdom of using loam or clay is very much questioned. When the latter material is used for a binder the road is apt to become very dusty in dry weather, and sticky, muddy, and rutty in wet weather.

The character of the foundation should never take the place of proper drainage. The advisability of underground or subdrainage should always be carefully considered where the road is liable to be attacked from beneath by water. In most cases good subdrains will so dry the foundation out that the macadam construction can be resorted to. Sometimes, however, thorough drainage is difficult or doubtful, and in such cases it is desirable to adopt some heavy construction like the telford; and, furthermore, the difficulty of procuring perfectly solid and reliable roadbeds in many places is often overcome by the use of this system.

In making a telford road the surface for the foundation is prepared in the same manner as for a macadam road. A layer of broken stone is then placed on the roadbed from five to eight inches in depth, depending upon the thickness to be given the finished road. As a rule this foundation should form about two-thirds of the total thickness of the material. The stone used for the first layer may vary in thickness from two to four inches and in length from eight to twelve inches. The thickness of the upper edges of the stones should not exceed four inches. They are set by hand on their broadest edges lengthwise across the road, breaking joints as much as possible. All projecting points are then broken off and the interstices or cracks filled with stone chips, and the whole structure wedged and consolidated into a solid and complete pavement. Upon this pavement layers of broken stones are spread and treated in the same way as for a macadam road.

Stone roads should be frequently scraped, so as to remove all dust and mud. Nothing destroys a stone road quicker than dust or mud. The hand method of scraping with a hoe is considered best. No matter how carefully adjusted the machinery built for this purpose may be, it is liable to ravel a road by loosening some of the stones. The gutters and surface drains should be kept open, so that all water falling upon the road or on the adjacent ground may promptly flow away. Says Spalding, a road authority:

"If the road metal be of soft material which wears easily, it will require constant supervision and small repairs whenever a rut or depression may appear. Material of this kind binds readily with new material that may be added, and may in this manner frequently be kept in good condition without great difficulty, while if not attended to at once when wear begins to show it will very rapidly increase, to the great detriment of the road. In making repairs by this method the material is commonly placed a little at a time and compacted by passing vehicles. The material used for this purpose should be the same as that of the road surface and not fine material, which would soon reduce to powder under the loads which come upon it. By careful attention to minute repairs in this manner a surface may be kept in good condition until it wears so thin as to require renewal.

"In case the road be of harder material, that will not so readily combine when a thin coating is added, repairs may not be frequent, as the surface will not wear so rapidly, and immediate attention is not so important. It is usually more satisfactory in this case to make more extensive repairs at one time, as a larger quantity of material added at once may be more readily compacted to a uniform surface, the repairs taking the form of an additional layer upon the road.

"Where the material of the road surface is very hard and durable, a well-constructed road may wear quite evenly and require hardly any attention, beyond ordinary small repairs, until worn out. It is now usually considered the best practice to leave such a road to itself until it wears very thin, and then renew it by an entirely new layer of broken stone placed on the worn surface and without in any way disturbing that surface.

"If a thin layer only of material is to be added at one time, in order that it may unite firmly with the upper layer of the road, it is usually necessary to break the bond of the surface material before placing the new layer, either by picking it up by hand or by a steam roller with short spikes in its surface, if such a machine is at hand. Care should be taken in doing this, however, that only the surface layer be loosened and that the solidity of the body of the road be not disturbed, as might be the case if the spikes are too long."

In repairing roads the time-honored custom of waiting until the road has lost its shape or until the surface has become filled with holes or ruts should never be tolerated. Much good material is wasted by spreading a thick coat over such a road and leaving it thus for passing vehicles to consolidate. The material necessary to replace defects in a road should be added when the necessities arise and should be of the best quality and the smallest possible quantity. If properly laid in small patches the inconvenience to traffic will be scarcely perceptible. If such repairs are made in damp weather, as they ought to be, little or no difficulty is experienced in getting a layer of stone to consolidate properly. If mud fills the rut or hole to be repaired, it should be carefully removed before the material is placed.

Wide tires should be used on all heavy vehicles which traverse stone roads. A four or five inch stone or gravel road will last longer without repair when wide tires are used than an eight or ten inch road of the same material on which narrow tires are used.

Not only should brush and weeds be removed from the roadside, but grass should be sown, trees planted, and a side path or walk be prepared for the use of pedestrians, especially women and children, going to and coming from church, school, and places of business and amusement. Country roads can be made far more useful and attractive than they usually are, and this may be secured by the expenditure of only a small amount of labor and money. Although such improvements are not necessary, they make the surroundings attractive and inviting and add to the value of property and the pleasure of the traveler.

If trees are planted alongside the road they should be far enough back to admit the wind and sun. Most strong growing trees are apt to extend their roots under the gutters and even beneath the roadway if they are planted too close to the roadside. Even if they be planted at a safe distance those varieties should be selected which send their roots downward rather than horizontally. The most useful and beautiful tree corresponding with these requirements is the chestnut, while certain varieties of the pear, cherry, and mulberry answer the same purpose. Where there is no danger of roots damaging the subdrainage or the substructure of the road, some other favorite varieties would be elms, rock maples, horse-chestnuts, beeches, pines, and cedars. Climate, variety of species selected, and good judgment will determine the distance between such trees. Elms should be thirty feet apart, while the less spreading varieties need not be so far. The trunks should be trimmed to a considerable height, so as to admit the sun and air. Fruit trees are planted along the roadsides in Germany and Switzerland, while mulberry trees may be seen along the roads in France, serving the twofold purpose of food for silkworms and shade. If some of our many varieties of useful, fruitful, and beautiful trees were planted along the roads in this country, and if some means could be devised for protecting the product, enough revenue could be derived therefrom to pay for the maintenance of the road along which they throw their grateful shade.

The improvement of country roads is chiefly an economical question, relating principally to the waste of effort in hauling over bad roads, the saving in money, time, and energy in hauling over good ones, the initial cost of improving roads, and the difference in the cost of maintaining good and bad ones. It is not necessary to enlarge on this subject in order to convince the average reader that good roads reduce the resistance to traffic, and consequently the cost of transportation of products and goods to and from farms and markets is reduced to a minimum.

The initial cost of a road depends upon the cost of materials, labor, machinery, the width and depth to which the material is to be spread on, and the method of construction. All these things vary so much in the different states that it is impossible to name the exact amount for which a mile of a certain kind of road can be built.

The introduction in recent years of improved road-building machinery has enabled the authorities in some of the states to build improved stone and gravel roads quite cheaply. First-class single-track stone roads, nine feet wide, have been built near Canandaigua, New York, for $900 to $1,000 per mile. Many excellent gravel roads have been built in New Jersey for $1,000 to $1,300 per mile. The material of which they were constructed was placed on in two layers, each being raked and thoroughly rolled, and the whole mass consolidated to a thickness of eight inches. In the same state macadam roads have been built, for $2,000 to $5,000 per mile, varying in width from nine to twenty feet and in thickness of material from four to twelve inches. Telford roads fourteen feet wide and ten to twelve inches thick have been built in New Jersey for $4,000 to $6,000 per mile. Macadam roads have been built at Bridgeport and Fairfield, Connecticut, eighteen to twenty feet wide, for $3,000 to $5,000 per mile. A telford road sixteen feet wide and twelve inches thick was built at Fanwood, New Jersey, for $9,500 per mile. Macadam roads have been built in Rhode Island, sixteen to twenty feet wide, for $4,000 to $5,000 per mile.

Massachusetts roads are costing all the way from $6,000 to $25,000 per mile. A mile of broken stone road, fifteen feet wide, costs in the state of Massachusetts about $5,700 per mile, while a mile of the same width and kind of road costs in the state of New Jersey only $4,700. This is due partly to the fact that the topography of Massachusetts is somewhat rougher than that of New Jersey, necessitating the reduction of many steep grades and the building of expensive retaining walls and bridges, and partly to the difference in methods of construction and the difference in prices of materials, labor, etc.

Doubtless the state of New Jersey is building more roads and better roads for less money per mile than any other state in the Union. Its roads are now costing from twenty to seventy cents per square yard. Where the telford construction is used they sometimes cost as much as seventy-three cents per square yard. The average cost of all classes of the roads of that state during the last season was about fifty cents per square yard. The stone was, as a rule, spread on to a depth of nine inches, which, after rolling, gave a depth of about eight inches. At this rate a single-track road eight feet wide costs about $2,346 per mile, while a double-track road fourteen feet wide costs about $4,106 per mile, and one eighteen feet wide costs about $5,280 per mile. Where the material is spread on so as to consolidate to a four-inch layer the eight-foot road will cost about $1,173 per mile, the fourteen-foot road about $2,053 per mile, while the one eighteen feet wide will cost about $2,640 per mile.

EARTH AND MACADAM ROADS

[Built by convict labor in Mecklenburg County, North Carolina]

The total cost of maintaining roads in good order ranges, on account of varying conditions, between as wide limits almost as the initial cost of construction. Suffice it to say that all money spent on repairing earth roads becomes each year a total loss without materially improving their condition. They are, as a rule, the most expensive roads that can be used, while on the other hand stone roads, if properly constructed of good material and kept in perfect condition, are the most satisfactory, the cheapest, and most economical roads that can be constructed.

The road that will best suit the needs of the farmer, in the first place, must not be too costly; and, in the second place, must be of the very best kind, for farmers should be able to do their heavy hauling over them when their fields are too wet to work and their teams would otherwise be idle.

The best road for the farmer, all things being considered, is a solid, well-built stone road, so narrow as to be only a single track, but having a firm earth road on one or both sides. Where the traffic is not very extensive the purposes of good roads are better served by narrow tracks than by wide ones, while many of the objectionable features of wide tracks are removed, the initial cost of construction is cut down one-half or more, and the charges for repair reduced in proportion.

FOOTNOTE:

[6] By Hon. Maurice O. Eldridge, Assistant Director Office of Public Road Inquiries.

CHAPTER IV

THE SELECTION OF MATERIALS FOR MACADAM ROADS[7]

No one rock can be said to be a universally excellent road material. The climatic conditions vary so much in different localities, and the volume and character of traffic vary so much on different roads, that the properties necessary to meet all the requirements can be found in no one rock. If the best macadam road be desired, that material should be selected which best meets the conditions of the particular road for which it is intended.

The movement for better country roads which has received such an impetus from the bicycle organizations is still felt, and is gaining force from the rapid introduction of horseless vehicles. To this demand, which comes in a large measure from the urban population, is to be added that of the farmer, who is wakening to the fact that good roads greatly increase the profits from his farm produce, and thus materially better his condition; and to the farmer, indeed, we must look for any real improvement in our country roads.

In considering the comparative values of different rocks for road-building, it must be taken for granted in all cases that the road is properly laid out, constructed, and maintained. For if this is not the case, only inferior results can be expected, no matter how good the material may be.

In most cases the selection of a material for road-making is determined more by its cheapness and convenience of location than by any properties it may possess. But when we consider the number of roads all over our country which are bad from neglect and from obsolete methods of maintenance that would be much improved by the use of any rock, this regard for economy is not to be entirely deprecated. At the same time, as a careless selection leads to costly and inferior results, too much care cannot be used in selecting the proper material when good roads are desired at the lowest cost. When macadam roads are first introduced into a district they are at worst so far superior to the old earth roads that the question is rarely asked, whether, if another material had been used, better roads would not have been obtained, and this at a smaller cost. When mistakes are made they are not generally discovered until much time and money have been expended on inferior roads. Such errors can in a great measure be avoided if reasonable care is taken in the selection of a suitable material. To select a material in a haphazard way, without considering the needs of the particular road on which it is to be used, is not unlike an ill person taking the nearest medicine at hand, without reference to the nature of the malady or the properties of the drug. If a road is bad, the exact trouble must first be ascertained before the proper remedy can be applied. If the surface of a macadam road continues to be too muddy or dusty after the necessary drainage precautions have been followed, then the rock of which it is constructed lacks sufficient hardness or toughness to meet the traffic to which it is subjected. If, on the contrary, the fine binding material of the surface is carried off by wind and rain and is not replaced by the wear of the coarser fragments, the surface stones will soon loosen and allow water to make its way freely to the foundation and bring about the destruction of the road. Such conditions are brought about by an excess of hardness or toughness of the rock for the traffic. Under all conditions a rock of high cementing value is desirable; for, other things being equal, such a rock better resists the wear of traffic and the action of wind and rain. This subject, however, will be referred to again.

Until comparatively recent years but little was known of the relative values of the different varieties of rock as road material, and good results were obtained more by chance and general observation than through any special knowledge of the subject. These conditions, however, do not obtain at present, for the subject has received a great deal of careful study, and a fairly accurate estimate can be made of the fitness of a rock for any conditions of climate and traffic.

In road-building the attempt should be made to get a perfectly smooth surface, not too hard, too slippery, or too noisy, and as free as possible from mud and dust, and these results are to be attained and maintained as cheaply as possible. Such results, however, can only be had by selecting the material and methods of construction best suited to the conditions.

In selecting a road material it is well to consider the agencies of destruction to roads that have to be met. Among the most important are the wearing action of wheels and horses' feet, frost, rain, and wind. To find materials that can best withstand these agencies under all conditions is the great problem that confronts the road-builder.

Before going further, it will be well to consider some of the physical properties of rock which are important in road-building, for the value of a road material is dependent in a large measure on the degree to which it possesses these properties. There are many such properties that affect road-building, but only three need be mentioned here. They are hardness, toughness, and cementing or binding power.

By hardness is meant the power possessed by a rock to resist the wearing action caused by the abrasion of wheels and horses' feet. Toughness, as understood by road-builders, is the adhesion between the crystal and fine particles of a rock, which gives it power to resist fracture when subjected to the blows of traffic. This important property, while distinct from hardness, is yet intimately associated with it, and can in a measure make up for a deficiency in hardness. Hardness, for instance, would be the resistance offered by a rock to the grinding of an emery wheel; toughness, the resistance to fracture when struck with a hammer. Cementing or binding power is the property possessed by the dust of a rock to act, after wetting, as a cement to the coarser fragments composing the road, binding them together and forming a smooth, impervious shell over the surface. Such a shell, formed by a rock of high cementing value, protects the underlying material from wear and acts as a cushion to the blows from horses' feet, and at the same time resists the waste of material caused by wind and rain, and preserves the foundation by shedding the surface water. Binding power is thus, probably, the most important property to be sought for in a road-building rock, as its presence is always necessary for the best results. The hardness and toughness of the binder surface more than of the rock itself represents the hardness and toughness of the road, for if the weight of traffic is sufficient to destroy the bond of cementation of the surface, the stones below are soon loosened and forced out of place. When there is an absence of binding material, which often occurs when the rock is too hard for the traffic to which it is subjected, the road soon loosens or ravels.

Experience shows that a rock possessing all three of the properties mentioned in a high degree does not under all conditions make a good road material; on the contrary, under certain conditions it may be altogether unsuitable. As an illustration of this, if a country road or city park way, where only a light traffic prevails, were built of a very hard and tough rock with a high cementing value, neither the best, nor, if a softer rock were available, would the cheapest results be obtained. Such a rock would so effectively resist the wear of a light traffic that the amount of fine dust worn off would be carried away by wind and rain faster than it would be supplied by wear. Consequently the binder supplied by wear would be insufficient, and if not supplied from some other source the road would soon go to pieces. The first cost of such a rock would in most instances be greater than that of a softer one and the necessary repairs resulting from its use would also be very expensive.

A very good illustration of this point is the first road built by the Massachusetts Highway Commission. This road is on the island of Nantucket and was subjected to a very light traffic. The commission desired to build the best possible road, and consequently ordered a very hard and tough trap rock from Salem, considered then to be the best macadam rock in the state. Delivered on the road this rock cost $3.50 per ton, the excessive price being due to the cost of transportation. The road was in every way properly constructed, and thoroughly rolled with a steam roller; but in spite of every precaution it soon began to ravel, and repeated rolling was only of temporary benefit, for the rock was too hard and tough for the traffic. Subsequently, when the road was resurfaced with limestone, which was much softer than the trap, it became excellent. Since then all roads built on the island have been constructed of native granite bowlders with good results, and at a much lower cost.

If, however, this hard and tough rock, which gave such poor results at Nantucket, were used on a road where the traffic was sufficient to wear off an ample supply of binder, very much better results would be obtained than if a rock lacking both hardness and toughness were used; for, in the latter case, the wear would be so great that ruts would be formed which would prevent rain water draining from the surface. The water thus collecting on the surface would soon make its way to the foundation and destroy the road. The dust in dry weather would also be excessive.

Only two examples of the misuse of a road material have been given, but, as they represent extreme conditions, it is easy to see the large number of intermediate mistakes that can be made, for there are few rocks even of the same variety that possess the same physical properties in a like degree. The climatic and physical conditions to which roads are subjected are equally varied. The excellence of a road material may, therefore, be said to depend entirely on the conditions which it is intended to meet.

It may be well to mention a few other properties of rock that bear on road-building, though they will not be discussed here. There are some rocks, such as limestones, that are hygroscopic, or possess the power of absorbing moisture from the air, and in dry climates such rocks are distinctly valuable, as the cementation of rock dust is in a large measure dependent for its full development on the presence of water. The degree to which a rock absorbs water may also be important, for in cold climates this to some extent determines the liability of a rock to fracture by freezing. It is not so important, however, as the absorptive power of the road itself, for if a road holds much water the destruction wrought by frost is very great. This trouble is generally due to faulty construction rather than to the material. The density or weight of a rock is also considered of importance, as the heavier the rock the better it stays in place and the better it resists the action of wind and rain.

Only a few of the properties of rock important to road builders have been considered, but if these are borne in mind when a material is to be selected better results are sure to be obtained. In selecting a road material the conditions to which it is to be subjected should first be considered. These are principally the annual rainfall, the average winter temperature, the character of prevailing winds, the grades, and the volume and character of the traffic that is to pass over the road. The climatic conditions are readily obtained from the Weather Bureau, and a satisfactory record of the volume and character of the traffic can be made by any competent person living in view of the road.

In France the measuring of traffic has received a great deal of attention, and a census is kept for all the national highways. The traffic there is rated and reduced to units in the following manner: A horse hauling a public vehicle or cart loaded with produce or merchandise is considered as the unit of traffic. Each horse hauling an empty cart or private carriage counts as one-half unit; each horse, cow, or ox, unharnessed, and each saddle horse, one-fifth unit; each small animal (sheep, goat, or hog), one-thirtieth unit.

A record is made of the traffic every thirteenth day throughout the year, and an average taken to determine its mean amount. Some such general method of classifying traffic in units is desirable, as it permits the traffic of a road to be expressed in one number.

Before this French method can be applied to the traffic of our country it will be necessary to modify considerably the mode of rating. This, however, is a matter which can be studied and properly adjusted by the Office of Public Road Inquiries. It is most important to obtain a record of the average number of horses and vehicles and kind of vehicles that pass over an earth road in a day before the macadam road is built. The small cost of such a record is trifling when compared with the cost of a macadam road (from $4,000 to $10,000 per mile for a fifteen-foot road), in view of the fact that an error in the selection of material may cost a much larger sum of money. After a record of the traffic is obtained, if the road is to be built of crushed rock for the first time, an allowance for an immediate increase in traffic amounting at least to ten or fifteen per cent had best be made, for the improved road generally brings traffic from adjoining roads.

To simplify the matter somewhat, the different classes of traffic to which roads are subjected may be divided into five groups, which may be called city, urban, suburban, highway, and country road traffic, respectively. City traffic is a traffic so great that no macadam road can withstand it, and is such as exists on the business streets of large cities. For such a traffic stone and wood blocks, asphalt, brick, or some such materials are necessary. Urban traffic is such as exists on city streets which are not subjected to continuous heavy teaming, but which have to withstand very heavy wear, and need the hardest and toughest macadam rock. Suburban traffic is such as is common in the suburbs of a city and the main streets of country towns. Highway traffic is a traffic equal to that of the main country roads. Country road traffic is a traffic equal to that of the less frequented country roads.

The city traffic will not be considered here. For an urban traffic, the hardest and toughest rock, or in other words, a rock of the highest wearing quality that can be found, is best. For a suburban traffic the best rock would be one of high toughness but of less hardness than one for urban traffic. For highway traffic a rock of medium hardness and toughness is best. For country road traffic it is best to use a comparatively soft rock of medium toughness. In all cases high cementing value should be sought, and especially if the locality is very wet or windy.

Rocks belonging to the same species and having the same name, such as traps, granites, quartzites, etc., vary almost as much in different localities in their physical road-building properties as they do from rocks of distinct species. This variation is also true of the mineral composition of rocks of the same species, as well as in the size and arrangement of their crystals. It is impossible, therefore, to classify rocks for road-building by simply giving their specific names. It can be said, however, that certain species of rock possess in common some road-building properties. For instance, the trap[8] rocks as a class are hard and tough and usually have binding power, and consequently stand heavy traffic well; and for this reason they are frequently spoken of as the best rocks for road-building. This, however, is not always true, for numerous examples can be shown where trap rock having the above properties in the highest degree has failed to give good results on light traffic roads. The reason trap rock has gained so much favor with road-builders is because a large majority of macadam roads in our country are built to stand an urban traffic, and the traps stand such a traffic better than any other single class of rocks. There are, however, other rocks that will stand an urban traffic perfectly well, and there are traps that are not sufficiently hard and tough for a suburban or highway traffic. The granites are generally brittle, and many of them do not bind well, but there are a great many which when used under proper conditions make excellent roads. The felsites are usually very hard and brittle, and many have excellent binding power, some varieties being suitable for the heaviest macadam traffic. Limestones generally bind well, are soft, and frequently hygroscopic. Quartzites are almost always very hard, brittle, and have very low binding power. The slates are usually soft, brittle, and lack binding power.

The above generalizations are of necessity vague, and for practical purposes are of little value, since rocks of the same variety occurring in different localities have very wide ranges of character. It consequently happens in many cases, particularly where there are a number of rocks to choose from, that the difficulty of making the best selection is great, and this difficulty is constantly increasing with the rapidly growing facilities of transportation and the increased range of choice which this permits. On account of their desirable road properties some rocks are now shipped several hundred miles for use.

There are but two ways in which the value of a rock as a road material can be accurately determined. One way, and beyond all doubt the surest, is to build sample roads of all the rocks available in a locality, to measure the traffic and wear to which they are subjected, and keep an accurate account of the cost both of construction and annual repairs for each. By this method actual results are obtained, but it has grave and obvious disadvantages. It is very costly (especially so when the results are negative), and it requires so great a lapse of time before results are obtained that it cannot be considered a practical method when macadam roads are first being built in a locality. Further than this, results thus obtained are not applicable to other roads and materials. Such a method, while excellent in its results, can only be adopted by communities which can afford the necessary time and money, and is entirely inadequate for general use.

The other method is to make laboratory tests of the physical properties of available rocks in a locality, study the conditions obtaining on the particular road that is to be built, and then select the material that best suits the conditions. This method has the advantages of giving speedy results and of being inexpensive, and as far as the results of laboratory tests have been compared with the results of actual practice they have been found to agree.

Laboratory tests on road materials were first adopted in France about thirty years ago, and their usefulness has been thoroughly established. The tests for rock there are to determine its degree of hardness, resistance to abrasion, and resistance to compression. In 1893 the Massachusetts Highway Commission established a laboratory at Harvard University for testing road materials. The French abrasion test was adopted, and tests for determining the cementing power and toughness of rock were added. Since then similar laboratories have been established at Johns Hopkins University, Columbia University, Wisconsin Geological Survey, Cornell University, and the University of California.

The Department of Agriculture has now established a road-material laboratory in the Division of Chemistry, where any person residing in the United States may have road materials tested free by applying for instructions to the 'Office of Public Road Inquiries. The laboratory is equipped with the apparatus necessary for carrying on such work, and the Department intends to carry on general investigations on roads. Part of the general plan will be to make tests on actual roads for the purpose of comparing the results with those obtained in the laboratory.

Besides testing road materials for the public, blank forms for recording traffic will be supplied by the department to any one intending to build a road.

When these forms are filled and returned to the laboratory, together with the samples of materials available for building the road, the traffic of the road will be rated in its proper group, as described above; each property of the materials will be tested and similarly rated according to its degree, the climatic conditions will be considered, and expert advice given as to the proper choice to be made.

FOOTNOTES:

[7] By Logan Waller Page, expert in charge of Road Material Laboratory, Division of Chemistry.

[8] This term is derived from the Swedish word *trappa*, meaning steps, and was originally applied to the crystallized basalts of the coast of Sweden, which much resemble steps in appearance. As now used by road builders, it embraces a large variety of igneous rocks, chiefly those of fine crystalline structure and of dark-blue, gray, and green colors. They are generally diabases, diorites, trachytes, and basalts. —PAGE.

CHAPTER V

STONE ROADS IN NEW JERSEY[9]

As New Jersey contains a great variety of soils, there are many conditions to be met with in road construction. The northern part of the state is hilly, where we have clay, soft stone, hard stones, loose stones, quicksand, and marshes. In the eastern part of the state, particularly in the seashore sections, the roads are at their worst in summer in consequence of loose, dry sand, which sometimes drifts like snow. In west New Jersey, which comprises the southern end of the state, there is much loose, soft sand, considerable clay, marshes, and low lands not easily drained.

In addition to the condition of the soil, there is the economic condition to be considered. In the vicinity of large towns or cities, where there is heavy carting by reason of manufactories and produce marketing, it is necessary to have heavy, thick, substantial roads, while in more rural districts and along the seashore, where the travel is principally by light carriages, a lighter roadbed construction is preferred. In rural districts, where the roads are used for immediate neighborhood purposes, an inexpensive road is desirable. The main thoroughfares have to be constructed with a view to considerable increase of travel, as farmers in the outlying districts who formerly devoted their time to grazing of stock, raising of grain, etc., find it more profitable to change the mode of farming to that of truck raising, fruit growing,etc.

The road engineers of New Jersey find that they cannot follow old paths and make their roads after one style or pattern. Technical engineering in road construction must yield to the practical, common-sense plan of action. An engineer with plenty of money and material at hand can construct a good road almost anywhere and meet any condition, but with limited resources and a variety of physical conditions he has to "cut the garment to suit the cloth." We start out with this dilemma. We must have better roads, and our means for getting them being very limited, if we cannot get them as good as we would like, let us get them as good as we can.

Let me give a practical illustration. Stone-road construction outside of turnpike corporations in West Jersey was begun in the spring of 1891. I was called on by the township committee of Chester Township, Burlington County, to construct some roads. Moorestown is a thriving town of about three thousand inhabitants in the center of the township. The roads to be constructed, with one exception, ran out of the town to the township limits, being from one-half to three miles in length. The roads were generally for local purposes. There were ten roads, aggregating about eleven miles. The bonding of the township was voted upon, and it was necessary, in order to carry the bonding project of $40,000, to have all these roads constructed of stone macadam. The roads to be improved were determined on at a town meeting without consulting an engineer as to the cost, etc., so that the plain question submitted to me was, Can you construct eleven miles of stone road nine feet wide for $40,000? The conditions to be met were these: There was no stone suitable for road-building nearer than from sixty to eighty miles; cost of freight, about seventy-five cents per ton; the hauls from the railroad siding averaged about one and three-quarter miles; price of teams in summer, when farmers were busy, about $3.50 per day. In preparation for road construction there were several hills to be cut from one to three feet; causeways and embankments to be made over wet and swampy ground. For this latter work the property holders and others interested along the road agreed to furnish teams, the township paying for laborers. The next difficulty was the kind of a road to build. As the width was fixed at nine feet as a part of the conditions for bonding, there seemed only one way left to apply the economics—that was, in the depth of the roads.

On the dry, sandy soils I put the macadam six inches deep; this depth was applied to about six miles of road. On roads where the heaviest travel would come the roadbed was made eight inches deep. On soils having springs and on embankments over causeways the depth was ten inches with stone foundation, known as telford. Where springs existed, they were cut off by underdrains.

It had been the practice of engineers in their specifications to call for the best trap rock for all the stone construction. As this rock is hard to crush and difficult to be transported some seventy or eighty miles to this part of New Jersey, I found that in order to construct all of the road from this best material it would take more money than the bonds would provide; so I had half of the depth which forms the foundation made of good dry sedimentary rock. Of course, in this there is considerable slate, but the breaking is not nearly so costly as the breaking of syenite or Jersey trap rock, and there was a saving of thirty per cent. As the surface of the road had to take all the wear, I required the best trap rock for this purpose.

Since the construction of these roads in Chester Township, roads are now built under the state-aid act by county officials and paid for as follows: One-third by the state, ten per cent by the adjoining property holders, and the balance (56-2/3 per cent) by the county. The roads constructed under this act are generally leading roads and those mostly traversed by heavy teams. They are constructed similarly to those in Chester Township, excepting that they are generally twelve feet wide and from ten to twelve inches deep. Many of them have a telford foundation, which is now put down at about the same price as macadam, and meets most of the conditions better than macadam. The less expensive stone is used for foundations, and the best and more costly for surface only. In this way the cost of construction has been greatly reduced.

In regard to the width, a road nine or ten feet wide has been found to be quite as serviceable as one of greater width, unless it is made fourteen feet and over. It is not claimed that a narrow road is just as good as a wide road, but it has been found better to have the cost in length than in width in rural districts. In and near towns, where there is almost constant passing, the road should not be less than from fourteen to twenty feet in width. The difficulty in getting on and off the stone road where teams are passing is not so great as is supposed. To meet this difficulty in the past, on each side of the road the specifications require the contractor to make a shoulder of clay, gravel, or other hard earth; this is never less than three feet and sometimes six to eight feet in width, according to the kinds of soil the road is composed of and the liability of frequent meeting and passing. In rural districts the top-dressing of these shoulders is taken from the side ditches; grass sods are mixed in when found, and in some cases grass seed is sown. As the stone roadbed takes the travel the grass soon begins to grow, receiving considerable fertilizing material from the washing of the road; and when the sod is once formed the waste material from the wear of the road is lodged in the grass sod and the shoulder becomes hard and firm, except when the frost is coming out.

Another mode of building a rural road cheaply and still have room for passing without getting off the stone construction is to make the roadbed proper about ten feet wide, ten or twelve inches deep; then have wings of macadam on each side three feet wide and five or six inches deep. In case ten feet is used the two wings would make the stone construction six feet wide. If the road is made considerably higher in the center than the sides, as it should be, the travel, particularly the loaded teams, will keep in the center, and the wings will only be used in passing and should last as long as the thicker part of the road.

The preparation of the road and making it suitable for the stone bed is one of the most important parts of road construction. This, once done properly, is permanent. Wherever it is possible the hills should be cut and low places filled, so that the maximum grade will not exceed five or six feet rise in one hundred feet; where hills cannot be reduced to this grade without incurring too much expense, the hill, if possible, should be avoided by relaying the road in another place.

Wherever stone roads have been constructed it has been found that those using them for drawing heavy loads will increase the capacity of their wagons so as to carry three or four times the load formerly carried. This can easily be done where the road has a maximum grade of not greater than five or six per cent, as before stated; but when the grade is greater than this the power to be expended on such loads upon such grades will exhaust and wear out the horses; thus a supposed saving in heavy loading may prove to be a loss.

In the preparation of the road it is necessary to have the ditches wide and deep enough to carry all the water to the nearest natural water way. These ditches should at all times be kept clear of weeds and trash, so that the water will not be retained in pools. Bad roads often occur because this important matter is overlooked.

On hills the slope or side grade in construction from center of road to side ditches should be increased so as to exceed that of the longitudinal grade; that is, if the latter is, say, five per cent, the slope to side should be at least six per cent and over.

Where the road in rural districts is on rolling ground and hills do not exceed three or four per cent, it is an unnecessary expense to cut the small ones, but all short rises should be cut and small depressions filled. A rolling road is not objectionable, and besides there is no better roadbed for laying on metal than the hard crust formed by ordinary travel. In putting on the metal, particularly on narrow roads, the roadbed should be "set high;" it will soon get "flat enough." It is better to put the shouldering up to the stone than to dig a trench to put the stone in. If the road after preparation is about level from side to side and the stone or metal construction is to be, say, ten inches deep, the sides of the roadbed to receive the metal should be cut about three inches and placed on the side to help form the shoulder; the rest of the shoulder, when suitable, being taken from the ditches and sides in forming the proper slope. The foundation to receive the metal, if the natural roadbed is not used and the bed is of soft earth, should be rolled until it is hard and compact. It should also conform to the same slope as the road when finished from center to sides. If the bed or foundation is of soft sand rolling will be of little use. In this case care must be taken to keep the bed as uniform as possible while the stone is being placed on the foundation.

When the road passes through villages and towns the grading should reduce the roadbed to a grade as nearly level as possible. It must be borne in mind that the side ditches need not necessarily always conform to the center grade of the road. When the center grade is level the side ditches should be graded to carry off the water. In some cases I have found it necessary to run the grade for the side ditches in an opposite direction from the grade of the road. This, however, does not often occur. The main thing is to get the water off the road as soon as possible after it falls, and then not allow it to remain in the ditches. And just here the engineer will meet with many difficulties. The landowners in rural districts are opposed to having the water from the roads let onto their lands, and disputes often arise as to where the natural water way is located. This should be determined by the people in the neighborhood, or by the local authorities. I have found in several cases, where the water from side ditches was allowed to run on the land, that the land was generally benefited by having the soil enriched by the fertilizing matter from the road.

After the roadbed has been thoroughly prepared, if made of loam or clay, it should be rolled and made as hard and compact as possible. Wherever a depression appears it should be filled up and made uniformly hard. Place upon it a light coat of loam or fine clay, which will act as a binder. If the roller used is not too heavy it may be rolled to advantage, but the rolling of this course depends upon the character of the stones. If the stones are cubical in form rolling is beneficial, but if they are of shale and many of them thin and flat, rolling has a tendency to bring the flat sides to the surface. When this is the case the next course of fine stone for the surface will not firmly compact and unite with them.

When the foundation is of telford it is important that stones not too large should be used. They should not exceed ten inches in length, six inches on one side, which is laid next to the earth, and four inches on top, the depth depending on the thickness of the road. If the thickness of the finished road is eight inches, the telford pavement should not exceed five inches; if it is ten or more inches deep, then the telford could be six inches. It need in no case be greater than this, as this is sufficient to form the base or foundation of the metal construction. The surface of the telford pavement should be as uniform as possible, all projecting points broken off, and interstices filled in with small stone. Care should be taken to keep the stone set up perpendicular with the roadbed and set lengthwise across the road with joints broken. This foundation should be well hammered down with sledge hammers and made hard and compact. Upon this feature greatly depends the smoothness of the surface of the road and uniform wear. If put down compactly rolling is not necessary, and if not put down solid rolling might do it damage in causing the large stones to lean and set on their edges instead of on the flat sides. I refer to instances where the road is to be ten inches and over. Then put on a light coat or course of one and one-half inch stone, with a light coat of binding, and then put on the roller, thus setting the finer stone well with the foundation and compacting the whole mass together.

After the macadam or telford foundation is well laid and compacted, the surface or wearing stone is put on. If the thickness of the road is great enough, say twelve or fourteen inches, this surface stone should be put on in courses, say of three and four inches, as may be required for the determined thickness of the road. On each course there should be applied a binding, but only sufficient to bind the metal together or fill up the small interstices. It must be remembered that broken stone is used in order to form a compact mass. The sides of the stone should come together and not be kept apart by what we call binding material; therefore only such quantity should be used as will fill up the small interstices made by reason of the irregularity of the stone. Each course should be thoroughly rolled to get the metal as compact as possible. When the stone construction is made to the required depth or thickness, the whole surface should be subjected to a coat of screenings about one inch thick. This must be kept damp by sprinkling, and thoroughly rolled until the whole mass becomes consolidated and the surface smooth and uniform. Before the rolling is finished the shoulders should be made up and covered with gravel or other hard earth and dressed off to the side ditches. When practicable these should have the same grade or slope as the stone construction. This finish should also be rolled and made uniform, so that, in order that the water may pass off freely, there will be no obstruction between the stone roadbed and side ditches. To prevent washes and insure as much hardness as possible on roads in rural districts, grass should be encouraged to grow so as to make a stiff sod.

For shouldering, when the natural soil is of soft sand, a stiff clay is desirable. When the natural soil is of clay, then gravel or coarse sand can be used, covering the whole with the ditch scrapings or other fertilizing material, where grass sod is desirable. Of course this is not desirable in villages and towns.

For binding, what is called garden loam is the best. When this cannot be found use any soft clay or earth free from clods or round stones. It must be spread on very lightly and uniformly.

Any good dry stone not liable to disintegrate can be used as metal for foundation for either telford or macadam construction. For the surface it is necessary to have the best stone obtainable. Like the edge of a tool, it does the service and must take the wear. As in the tool it pays to have the best of steel, so on the road, which is subject to the wear and tear of steel horseshoes and heavy iron tires, it is found the cheapest to have the best of stone.

It is difficult to describe the kind of stone that is best. The best is generally syenite trap rock, but this term does not give any definite idea. The kind used in New Jersey is called the general name of Jersey trap rock. It is a gray syenite, and is found in great quantities in a range running from Jersey City, on the Hudson River, to a point on the Delaware between Trenton and Lambertville. There are quantities of good stone lying north of this ledge, but none south of it.

The best is at or near Jersey City. The same kind of stone is found in the same ranges of hills in Pennsylvania, but in the general run it is not so good. The liability to softness and disintegration increases after leaving the eastern part of New Jersey, and while good stone may be found, the veins of poorer stone increase as we go south and west.

It is generally believed that the hardest stones are best for road purposes, but this is not the case. The hard quartz will crush under the wheels of a heavy load. It is toughness in the stone that is necessary; therefore a mixed stone, like syenite, is the best. This wears smooth, as the rough edges of the stone come in contact with the wheels. It requires good judgment based on experience to determine the right kind of stone to take the constant wear of horseshoes and wagon tires.

If good roads are desired, the work is not done when the road is completed and ready for travel. There are many causes which make repairing necessary. I will refer to only a few of them. Stone roads are liable to get out of order because of too much water or want of water; also, when the natural roadbed is soft and springy and has not been sufficiently drained; when water is allowed to stand in ditches and form pools along the road, and when the "open winters" give us a superabundance of wet. Before the road becomes thoroughly consolidated by travel it is liable to become soft and stones get loose and move under the wheels of the heavily loaded wagons. In the earth foundation on which the stone bed rests the water finds the soft spots. The wheels of the loaded teams form ruts, and particularly where narrow tires are used.

The work of repair should begin as soon as defects appear, for, if neglected, after every rain the depressions make little pools of water and hold it like a basin. In every case this water softens the material, and the wagon tires and horseshoes churn up the bottoms of the basins. This is the beginning of the work of destruction. If allowed to go on, the road becomes rough, and the wear and tear of the horses and wagons are increased. Stone roads out of repair, like any common road in similar condition, will be found expensive to those who use and maintain them. The way to do is to look over a road after a rain, when the depressions and basins will show themselves. Whenever one is large enough to receive a shovelful of broken stone, scrape out the soft dirt and let it form a ring around the depression. Fill with broken stone to about an inch or two above the surface of the road. The ring of dirt around will keep the stone above the surface in place, and the passing wheels will work it on the broken stone and also act as a binder. The whole will work down and become compact and even with the road surface. The ruts are treated in the same way. Use one and one-half inch stone for this; smaller stones will soon grind up and the hole appear again.

The second cause of the necessity for road repairs is want of water. This occurs in summer during hot, dry spells. The surface stone "unravels;" that is, becomes loose where the horses travel. This condition is more liable to be found on dry, sandy soils, and where the roadbed is subject to the direct rays of the sun, and where the winds sweep off all the binding material from the surface. In clay soil there is little or no trouble from "unraveling." The cause being found, the remedy is applied in this way: Put on water with the sprinkler before all the binding material is blown off. If the hot, dry weather continues, sprinkling should continue. Do this in the evening or late in the afternoon.

The next mode is to repair the road by placing the material back as it was originally. The loose stones are placed in the depressions and good binding material—garden loam or fine clay—is put on, then roll the whole repeatedly and dampen by sprinkling as needed until the whole surface becomes smooth and hard. Care must be taken that too much binding material is not used. If too much is used it will injure the road in winter when there is an excess of water.

When a road has been neglected and allowed to become uneven and rough, or is by constant use worn down to the foundation stones, there should be a general repairing. In the first place, if it is the roughness and unevenness that is the only defect, this may be remedied by the use of a large, heavy roller with steel spikes in its rolling wheels. This will puncture the surface so that an ordinary harrow will tear up the surface stones. Then take the spikes out of the roller wheels, and, with sprinkling and rolling, the roadbed can be repaired and made like a new road. But if the cause of the roughness is from wearing away of the stone, so that the surface of the road is brought down to or near the foundation, then the road needs resurfacing. The mode of treatment is the same as in the other case.

In districts where there is stone suitable for road construction the county, town, township, or other municipality, proposing to construct stone roads, should own a stone quarry and a stone crusher. For grading and preparing the road for construction, dressing up sides, clearing out side ditches, etc., a good road machine is necessary. For constructing roads and repairing them a roller is necessary, the weight depending upon the kind of road constructed. If the road is not wide a roller of from four to six tons is all the weight necessary. The rolling should be continued until compactness is obtained. For wide, heavy roads a steam roller of fifteen tons can be used to advantage. A sprinkling wagon completes the list that is necessary for the county or town or other municipality constructing its own roads.

Lightning Source UK Ltd.
Milton Keynes UK
UKHW012001020822
406760UK00002B/38